PENGUIN BOOKS

POWDERED EGGS

A former editor of *The New York Times Book Review*, Charles Simmons is the author of three other novels: *The Belles Lettres Papers, An Old-Fashioned Darling,* and *Wrinkles*, all available from Penguin. *Powdered Eggs* received the William Faulkner Award for a notable first novel. Charles Simmons resides in New York City and on eastern Long Island.

charles simmons

POWDERED EGGS

a novel

PENGUIN BOOKS

PENGUIN BOOKS
Published by the Penguin Group
Viking Penguin Inc., 40 West 23rd Street,
New York, New York 10010, U.S.A.
Penguin Books Ltd, 27 Wrights Lane,
London W8 5TZ, England
Penguin Books Australia Ltd, Ringwood,
Victoria, Australia
Penguin Books Canada Ltd, 2801 John Street,
Markham, Ontario, Canada L3R 1B4
Penguin Books (N.Z.) Ltd, 182–190 Wairau Road,
Auckland 10, New Zealand

Penguin Books Ltd, Registered Offices:
Harmondsworth, Middlesex, England

First published in the United States of America by E. P. Dutton 1964
Published in Penguin Books 1988

1 3 5 7 9 10 8 6 4 2

LIBRARY OF CONGRESS CATALOGING IN PUBLICATION DATA
Simmons, Charles, 1924–
Powdered eggs: a novel/Charles Simmons.
p. cm.
ISBN 0 14 00.3201 0
I. Title.
PS3569.I4279P6   1988
813'.54 — dc19   88-9610

Printed in the United States of America by
R. R. Donnelley & Sons Company, Harrisonburg, Virginia
Set in Linotype Waldbaum

To HELEN FITZGERALD

POWDERED EGGS

❋ ❋ ❋ ❋ ❋ ❋ ❋ ❋ ❋ THE HEN GETS cocked, a great experience in itself. The egg-making mechanism takes the initial ingredients, mixes them for a time with digested chicken feed, fashions the white and yellow into a nice balance, wraps it in a shell. Plop. But instead of another chicken, a guy comes along, snatches the egg, bangs out the contents, sucks up the juice, puts the nasty powder into an envelope, marks it air mail, sends it to you, you add water, heat and eat. All alien to the orginal process and purpose. I mean, even if it tasted like something! Everything swirls around me, also in a kind of balance, and I reduce it to a few hundred words, mark it air mail and send it out to you. I told you about this male-type fag instructor at school. Nice guy really. But a poor baby. Talks about faking an orgasm with his wife. Harvey said he met him in the pisseria one day, and the guy went to great lengths to explain how wrong people were to think peckers were dirty. His pecker was the cleanest part of his body. Anyway, this guy's going off next semester to be headmaster of a fancy boys' school in New England, and he offered me a job there, except that I have to have an M.A. Duffy told him I have a great talent, which is so. Right after you left, Duffy brought one of my stories into class and read it, the one about the guy who couldn't laugh. I had handed it in for the senior fiction contest. Anyway, you know how Duffy runs that course, passes around mimeographed copies of stories with no author. This day he apologizes for not having had copies made and just reads. It wasn't until he was a quarter through, that I realized it was mine. I thought it was somebody else's story I knew by heart. Then, get this, he reads a Chekhov story and goes on to conduct a discussion about Story One and Story Two, Writer One and Writer Two. I lost, Chekhov beat me, which was as it should be. I mean, I didn't talk to anyone for a week as it was. But really, I remember walking down along the river that afternoon, being Writer One. So I have a great talent, but what do I know from fancy boys' schools in New England? I was pleased to be asked, you understand. You have your own house on the grounds, six M per annum, or is it anus? I said Maybe. But the M.A. Did Harvey tell you about his M.A. experience? He showed up at the initial seminar, run under the guidance of a wall-eyed grad-school prof, who kept saying Indeed. So wall-eyed that no one at the conference table knew whom he was addressing. Much confusion, and when Harvey said he wanted to do a translation of Catullus for his thesis, the guy coughed and said that Catullus had already been translated into English, a number of times. I don't think he's been well translated, Harvey said. Well, said the wall-eyed cougher, if you should produce the best translation of Catullus in English it would indeed be acceptable for a degree, but isn't that rather taking a chance? You see, he went on, we must try to make a contribution to the history of ideas. For instance, if you care to describe the important occurrences of a certain year in a certain place—1712 in London, say—that would indeed be a contribution to the history of ideas. Many years and places have been covered. Many others are indeed still open. I mean, talk about powdered eggs! You didn't take General Psychology, did you? I thought it was going to be full of wet libido. Instead the department had fallen into the hands of the behaviorists, guys with the dedication of Chinese Communists. Charting, charting, charting the responses of caged rats to various stimuli. And rats were only the beginning. The department head addressed us one day, he must have been carried away (he should have been), because he confessed that the behaviorist's mission was someday to chart all the possible human responses to all possible stimuli. Then, he said, the human psyche would be an open book. Harvey stood up and suggested that the book might prove unwieldy. The bastards gave him a C, which screwed Phi Beta Kappa for him. Me too. If Duffy hadn't gone on leave I would have had one. But screw it. Who cares? I care. Anyway, did I tell you I was sitting in the cafeteria with Harvey and two other guys—I don't think you know them—and we started talking about Phi Beta Kappa keys. I said if I got one I'd wear it under my foreskin, which I noticed at the time kind of stopped conversation. Later Harvey said that was a very snotty-clever remark I had made. What remark, I said. About the foreskin. Were you unaware of the religious persuasion of our two companions, he asked. You know,

I felt very bad about that, and the next time I met one of them I tried to explain that I had meant no offense, but he gave me the freeze. For Chrissake, it could make one anti-semantic. I mean, powdered eggs, man! Anyway, this male-type fag instructor and I got to talking about jobs. He was complaining how low-paying the academic life was and said that, off campus, he moved with a theatrical crowd, producers, directors, and such. That's where the money is, he said. Or some of it. The rest, according to him, was spread among his nonworking kin. It seems he's the only poor member (sic) of an illustrious American banking family. Do you know how much money is lost on a stage flop, he said. Two, three hundred thousand. Anyone who could tell hits from flops beforehand could make a fortune for himself. I can do that, I said. He looked at me, profoundly, mystically, and said How? Well, I said, I'd read the play first. Yes, yes, he said. I'd read the play first, and then if I liked it it would be a hit. If I didn't like it it would be a flop. This knocked him out, because after a silence he began to mumble, Maybe you can, maybe you can. Go down to see my friend at the Burton Shotwell Agency and tell him you can do this. Tell hits from flops, I asked. Yes, and tell him I said you can do it. How about the job in the boys' school, I said. The hell with that, he said, you can make a fortune in the theater, what do you want to teach for? Which made sense, and he gave me the guy's name and even said he'd call him up beforehand. So today I went down to the Burton Shotwell Agency. Tremendous waiting room. Big horseshoe desk at one end, inside of which was the second-most-beautiful woman I have ever seen, the receptionist. Without looking at me—I mean, she looked over me, under me, through me—she told me to sit down and wait. I was splendiferous, she didn't know what she was missing. And the splendor I bore was that gabardine sports jacket and a great pair of Oxford-gray English flannel slacks I got for twelve bucks, pressed to a cutting edge. I too was beautiful, I fit right in. Around this big room, along the wall, was a leather-cushioned bench, and opposite me, seated thereon, fine legs crossed, was the first-most-beautiful woman I have ever seen, reading. Walking up and down in front of her, paying no heed, was the first-most-beautiful man I have ever seen, also reading. I sat and pondered. How come these two delicious persons do not fall into each other's arms and raise the world's beauty quotient? After much thought I discovered why. They were actors. Anyway, I was much impressed, and their dumb show distracted me as I waited. Waited, O Christ, how I waited, feeling infinitely sorry for myself, until I chanced to look down, and there in my lap my fly bloomed. Dilemma. Should I brave out the interview thus, risking the loss of a fortune, or should I try to do myself up, chancing that these three beautiful people would think I was a pervert? After anguish I decided to invest the present in the future, and with one quick and agile flip I zippered up the jewels. Had I unconsciously been trying to appeal to the male-type fag's friend, or have I just been reading too much neo-Freud? Anyway, the three beautiful people couldn't have cared less, wherein lies a moral, which I leave to your definition. At last I was summoned. Extrapolating from the size of the reception room, I expected the male-type fag's friend's office to be de trop, the guy himself in front of a large window behind a mahogany desk, carpets and a bar and Picassos on the wall. Actually he was crouched over a metal desk in his shirt sleeves, and beside him with the tip of her can on the edge of a chair was a secretary taking dictation. Grandly I stood in the doorway. He looked up, the secretary looked up. I announced my name. Yes, he said. I announced it again, as if it had meaning. Yes, he said. I reminded him that probably his friend had called about me. Still he said Yes, and the secretary gave an impatient twitch with her can. I came to read plays, I said. His face eased. Have you got a girl, he said. What, I said. His face tightened. Have you got a girl? Yes, I said. Which was a lie, I haven't seen Mary for three weeks. But I thought the guy wanted to know whether I was straight, especially since I had been recommended by the male-type fag. So, Yes, I said. Where is she? This question I didn't understand. At home I guess, I said. The secretary twitched her can again. How can you read if she's at home, he said. Well, the three of us hung on this question for longer than I care to remember, until finally it was me that understood what was going on. O you think I'm an actor, I'm not an actor, I came to read plays to see if they would be hits or flops. It sounded wretched, saying it out like that, but, after all, that was the case. The bastard made me repeat it. I came to read plays to see if they would be hits or flops, I said. Well, the can twitched, and he drew his hand across his face like sandpaper on a board. I do that, he said, Mr. Shotwell does that. And I left. I mean, I thanked him and I left. What can I say?

✼ ✼ ✼ ✼ ✼ ✼ ✼ ✼ MY FATHER DIED. He was buried today. At the moment I'm here alone with my mother. My father had a heart attack ten days ago. He and my mother were coming back from playing bridge with two friends, and the thing began in the cab on the way. This one was bad. I mean, not only because my father finally died, but they knew it was bad even before. The doctor said my father possibly had a previous attack that hadn't been recognized as one. Or maybe he had one and never told us about it, which would be like him. You know the old line about never sick a day in his life. Well, that was my father in a way. He was never sick in bed. But he looked lousy for, I guess, years. He was seventy-one. He was forty-nine when I was born and in many ways not a father. He seemed old to me even when I was a kid, more like my mother's father than mine. Anyway, let me tell you what happened, and bear with me. If I was on with Mary I don't think I'd be writing this. But I feel very much alone. My mother is in bed, it's one A.M., and I'm out in the kitchen with the door closed, so she can't hear the typing. I've got six cans of beer to see me through this, and if it gets too much for you, open a bottle and send me the bill. Well, on the night of the attack I was out and got home late. My mother had had the doctor, he had given my father an electrocardiogram and told her it was a heart attack. Now get this. My father didn't get into the hospital until four o'clock the next afternoon. This crummy doctor is associated, as they say, with one of those private profit-making hospitals, and there wasn't an empty bed at the moment. The doctor claimed it didn't matter, that he was doing all they would do at the hospital, which turned out not to be the case, but anyway that's what he said. So my father was awake and asleep all through the night and next day, from sedatives, and the poor bastard kept talking about the pains in his hands. Even his finger tips hurt, he said, and he didn't seem to understand how it could hurt him down to his finger tips. Well, finally two clowns showed up with a stretcher on wheels and wrap-around blankets like a shroud, and we shoved off. My father was pretty low by that time. I was sitting right there next to him in the ambulance, and he asked my mother where I was. And then—Jesus, it's hard to be-lieve—we waited in the lobby of the goddamned hospital for twenty minutes while the room was being fixed up. People walking in and out, nurses, doctors, visitors, pa-tients, and there was my father on the stretcher on the floor, wide awake now, embarrassed or confused or some-thing, and all I could think of was the hundred thousand times he had taken us out to dinner or a play, or anything really, and it was always the best. You never met him, but he was kind of a distinguished-looking man. Everybody moved for him. And here he was, brought low, in the hands of some neighborhood jerk doctor, in some neighborhood jerk hospital, waiting on the floor for his life to be saved. If it was me on the floor he would have made them move. Christ, we wouldn't have been in this crummy little death factory to begin with. I remember when I was a kid and had my appendix out, how it was zip zip, the best room, the best nurses, the best surgeon—the guy who discovered the appendix or something—and here I stood at the admittance desk whining politely while the jerk clerk assured me that everything was being attended to as quickly as was humanly possible. Well anyway, when we finally got him into a room the house quack, a guy with an accent who looked like he thought he was too good for the job, took my father's blood pressure, which was down to about nothing, and ordered this and that, a bottle on a hook with a needle dripping into a vein, and a nurse to take my father's blood pressure every ten minutes, that sort of thing. Anyway, he came around. His blood pressure went up, and they took out the needle and gave him some more dope and by ten o'clock the next morning he was asleep and still alive. Before I left, the neighborhood jerk doctor showed up, looking fresh and rested, and asked if I wanted an oxygen tent for my father. I stared at him. I mean, who was running the show? I don't know, I said, should he have an oxygen tent? He pursed his lips and nodded diagonally. I didn't get it. I mean, I really thought this jerk was asking for my medical opinion, and finally I realized it was money. What could I do to reassure him? I mean, I wanted to stroke his cheek and say Please, please don't worry about money. Please get oxygen. Please get radium. Well, I got over to him, I guess. But it made me think, because here we were living in a nice place, the same building as the doctor himself. We have lived there a long time, so obviously we paid the rent, and the doctor knew it was a high rent. So what did this question mean, in terms of the doctor's experience? Well, it meant either a lot of people with dough tighten up when the provider can't sign the checks any more, or else it meant that a lot of people live nice and never have an extra dime around. I don't know what oxygen costs, but if oxygen makes one thousandth part of one thousandth part of a small difference, would anybody not buy it for his father? Apparently. Anyway, it shook me. I didn't like this creepy little jerk doctor to start with, so that morning after I left the hospital I went to see the head of the physiology department at school and asked him who the best cardiologist in the city was. A guy named Newman. I called him up and he came to the hospital as a consultant that afternoon. You ought to see the jerk doctor scrape and bow and sir him. Dr. Newman told me my father had a fifty-fifty chance, and the more time that passed, the better the chance would become. But I watched him with my father. He was great, Newman, and my old man saw the quality. He had felt demeaned, just as I had, in the hands of the local jerk. O Jesus, maybe I shouldn't be putting this guy down. I tell you why. Newman must have seen I was unsure, because he told me the guy was a good doctor and had done the right things. But I wanted the best. That's understandable, isn't it? To want the best for your father? When I was a kid and he took me downtown to get my suits we went to the boys' department of the same store he went to, and he'd get his own salesman to oversee the operation. They moved for him, my father. He wasn't an educated man. He only finished grammar school and then went to work and occasionally he said don't when he should have said doesn't, but he impressed people. He had the mark on him. He had a sense of his own dignity. He was steady-on, you know what I mean? He retired six years ago, but he used to go down to meet his business friends once in a while for lunch, and sometimes I went along, and I saw how they treated him, even though he was out of the line and an old man. They listened to him. He had the mark on him, and I'm glad I got him the goddamned cardiologist. Well, I spent a lot of time at the hospital. Every day that passed, the chances got better, so that by the time he died I was sure he'd recover. It was about eleven o'clock in the morning and my mother called me from the hospital. My father had taken a turn for the worse and maybe I should come up. I knew he was dead. I mean, I knew it and I didn't know it. If you're on the edge and you take a turn for the worse, you're dead, aren't you? But I didn't press it, I told my mother I'd be right up. Well, it seems she was waiting for me at the front entrance, but I went in the back and walked up to my father's floor. As soon as I saw his door was closed I was sure. But I wasn't sure either. I asked the head nurse to see him. O, she said, and went off to confer with another nurse, and they hemmed and hawed and finally they told me he was dead, and I burst out crying. One dopey nurse said Your father must have been a very good man, but she looked uncomfortable, with her eyes shifting like she wanted to be somewhere else, and I could have kicked her in the mons veneris. Well, I stood there blubbering and this little colored nurse came from the other end of the hall and put my head on her shoulder, and she understood, and I slobbered on her for a while. I pulled myself together and went downstairs, and there was my mother. She and I patted each other on the back for a while, but all the tears were gone, and we talked and went home. We went to the bank and brought back the contents of the safe-deposit box, the will and bonds and a lot of stuff, so the Revenue Department wouldn't seal it up. I knew the will left everything to my mother, my father told me that when he made me executor on my birthday five months ago, but I expected some message. That's what I wanted my father to leave me. Something, even some corn like To thine own self be true, or A rolling stone gathers no moss. But nothing, just legal jerk talk. Anyway, there's a lot of money, so my mother doesn't have to worry, and neither does the oxygen company, I'm glad to say. In the afternoon I went to the funeral home. I expected this to be the bottom, some unctuous professional asshole expressing his sorrow and all. But it wasn't. The guy I talked to was all right, quiet and human, and the next day we began the vigil. Either my mother or I was there from ten in the morning till ten at night for two days. Friends of my parents and their grown children, my friends, relatives—a few I had never seen before—all came. Some were very sorry my father had died, some were sorry that anybody had died, some were neutral and philosophical, and some were inwardly reassured, as if there was a certain quantity of death to go around and now their own chances were a little better for a little while. But I dug it. It was a long, sleepless, exhausting time, but it was good for us, at least for me. We were able to do something, able to use ourselves up. Exactly what my father died of you couldn't tell without an autopsy. Either he had another heart attack, or his heart burst or just stopped. But anyway, it seems that right before he died he couldn't talk, a nurse was in the room, and he took a pencil and paper and wrote Get the . . . , and then he died. Well, my uncle, my mother's brother, was convinced that the missing word was priest, and he kept the piece of paper with him to show to people that came to the funeral home. I don't know why this should have irritated me so, but it did. I mean, it's possible my father wanted a priest. But I doubt it. He was a Protestant, you know. My mother was the Catholic, and as a result religion was never discussed in the house. I was sent to a Catholic grammar school, but unlike the other kids I wasn't completely surrounded by Catholicism. In the fifth grade the nun asked if anyone in the class had a non-Catholic parent. When I confessed, she called me up and told me it was my duty to pray for my father's conversion. Well, maybe some priest told my uncle that too, and maybe he's been praying all these years, and maybe his prayers were finally answered, but I'd be sorry to know they had been. You see, my father was the avenue to another world for me. He was proof that non-Catholics were human beings. You have no idea the strange notions Catholics are imbued with. There is a secret understanding among Catholics that non-Catholics are, not evil or wrong-minded or ill-willed particularly, but terribly misguided. Protestants especially. And as for pagans, Asian babies and such, why they're raw material for the machine. Catholics are like Communists in this, I guess, except that they haven't been doing so well lately. In fact, that's why Catholics get excited about communism. It disturbs their dreams of progress in the propagation of the faith. I'd say that Catholics are like Jews too, except that Jews are desperate to maintain their exclusivity. Sometimes I think the worst thing that could happen to Jews would be for everybody to become a Jew. Who'd be left to crap on them then? Who'd be left to be better than? But Catholics, Jaysus! Well, the very word catholic tells the story. Anyway, my uncle kept this paper to show to visitors. I'd watch him from across the room, and I'd see the furrowed brows on the people as they studied the paper and then their intensity as they listened to his explanation, and finally the noddings of agreement when he'd spring the snapper, Get the . . . priest! I couldn't stand it. It wasn't my uncle's foolishness that bothered me, it was that my father was being defined in absentia. He never went to church, Catholic or Protestant, for as long as I knew him. That was the life he led, and why now at the close his brother-in-law had to ascribe to him a failure of nerve and sense I couldn't understand. Anyway, after he did his stuff for the tenth time, I went over and asked him for the paper to show to someone. I took it to the funeral director's office and filled in the word bedpan. Then I gave it back to him. Inside of ten minutes he had it out again. The guy he showed it to didn't laugh or anything, but did he looked puzzled! Today when my uncle came home with us for a while I sneaked the paper out of his pocket and flushed it down the toilet. But my sad story's not done. The services were a problem. Since my father wasn't connected with any church in a going way, we decided to ask the minister from the nearest Episcopalian parish to come. No speeches, just a prayer and whatever. I was surprised how alien he looked. I mean, a priest I would have been at home with. Even some red-faced Irish slob or midget wop I would have understood. I'd have felt he was representing something—something false, it's true—but in its way something sincere. But this minister! In the first place he looked like a young God the Father, and I've never had much use for God the Father. Big, about thirty-five, with a great head of live white hair. Impressive, but as I said, alien. Tremendous vacuous mush, the kind of mush Billy Graham stirs the gallstones of old ladies with. Something was wrong, I mean objectively wrong. Here this guy had come to do the dirty deed, and he was a stranger to my father. I wanted him to know something about the man he was burying, as if he had actually ministered to him in his life. So I went up and introduced myself. He turned his big benign smile on me, and I said My father wasn't a religious man but he was a moral man, and I started to cry. The tears came pouring out, and do you know what this big oaf did? Nothing. He just kept on smiling as if I had told him I had a cold. Well, I got away and went to the can and I was furious. I mean, a priest—the cruddiest, drunkenest, faggiest priest —would have responded. Would have made a sign, not of compassion or anything like that necessarily, but a sign that he understood. Not this character, however. O he did the bit later, which I'm sure impressed all the Catholics in the audience. Did it suavely, and I thought to myself So this is what Protestants hire to guide them along life's perilous paths. Get the bedpan, man.

✖ ✖ ✖ ✖ ✖ NOTE THE NEW ADDRESS. Two Hungarian engineers are living, and I mean living, at the old. My mother decided to break it up and move in with her brother. She gave me five thousand bucks and suggested that I set up for myself. I never expected that she wouldn't want to hang on, not to the apartment, but to me. She took her life in her hand, however, and said I'm going here, you go there. I experienced a catalogue of responses. At first I thought she was doing it because she thought I wanted it, but when I inquired of myself whether I wanted it or not I found I didn't particularly. In fact I felt dumped from the nest somewhat. Then what in all modesty I can only describe as my good sense came into play, and I decided that regardless of what she really wanted and I really wanted, this was a good thing. And so it's turned out. Two and a half furnished rooms. The big room is big, about fifteen by twenty, flat white, with two great windows that rise from under my knees to way over my head. An arched passage and waist-high counter separate the kitchen, which actually is just the essentials lined up one beside the other. The bedroom is squeezed, but has the same high ceiling and one of the same windows as the living room. I still haven't gotten used to the furniture. It's not only that the chairs and table and sofa and bed and rugs are old, I don't mind that, it's that they haven't acquired my smell yet. They're still in transition between the previous occupant and me. Who he was, I don't know. I guess it was a he, because there's an elaborate, lovingly rendered original drawing of the known atomic particles on the wall. I can't imagine why anyone would leave it. Or maybe it didn't belong to the previous occupant, maybe it just comes with the room. It has a Blakean quality, as if it was intended to be an absolute statement of some sort about the universe. I'm leaving it up to remind myself that from just such dust did I come and to just such dust shall I return. So what's this loneliness people talk about? Jaysus, to rise and fall at will, how glorious! And when I say fall I mean flop, clothed or naked, drunk or sober, whenever. And by rise I mean erect the monster to enormous heights, thus to fascinate the wondering wandering eye of yonder nuns across the street crouching behind half-drawn shades in the darkness of their celibate cells. Hey, I bought a six-year-old Austin-Healey. Paint worn, leather cracked, windows passing through the last stages of translucency into the beginnings of opacity. Nine hundred dollars, from a Filipino doctor. The poor bastard cried when he signed over the registration, so I guess it's in good shape. Shakes like a washing machine from sixty-four to seventy-two, the sound barrier, but afterward is a marble on glass. Speed seems to straighten what needs straightening and center what needs centering. I had it up to ninety-seven, wanted to put it over a hundred, just to say I'd been there, but I lost my nerve. Did you know I was a coward? Yeah, you knew it, but I didn't. It kind of amuses me. I mean, I always thought of myself as a hero. Anyway, you should have seen the two subletting Hungarians. They looked like brothers, curly-headed popeyed buckos. Very proper in front of my mother, but when I went back to get my books one of them told me they were setting up with a chocolate chick of their acquaintance. It seems they had both been pushing her, neither knowing about the other, and when they found out, instead of being pissed off, they decided to get a bigger place and take her in. The neighbors will love it. Maybe I should have warned them to dress her up as the maid. On the other hand maybe they should learn about the American Way by themselves. Actually they're charming guys, they might even prove so guiltless about the arrangement as to actually get away with it. And you want to hear something funny, I was sure my old lady would be outraged if she knew their intentions, but later she told me that she had gathered from the looks they gave each other when inspecting the apartment that they planned to have a time for themselves. Me? Well— but wait. Where's your letter? I'm not going to pour myself into this typewriter unless you recip, man. I'm not writing for posterity or prosperity. You wouldn't be pissed off at what I said about Protestants, would you? I mean, Protestants are fair game. I grant you, when Kennedy was elected there might have been reason for some slight sensitivity, but fellahs, you still got the country by the cunt. So take it, don't Protest. Me, I've gotten and lost a job. For two weeks I was a Writer, and here's how. Harvey got himself hired by a company that is revising a multivolume, defunct encyclopedia, the Modern Universal International Encyclopedia. Ever hear of it? Of course not. It was never much, I mean even when it was new, which was screwteen years ago and since then it's been given away volume by volume in movie lobbies and supermarkets, exchanged for six mills and two boxtops, sold by weight, confiscated for back taxes, plundered for items to fill the bottom of New Yorker columns, like The belief that goats eat tin cans is widespread but false and probably arises from the fact that goats eat the labels of tin cans with relish. Anyway, this company bought the property and is sinking half a million into revising it. I'm told that half a million isn't much to re-do an encyclopedia, but it seemed like a lot when I learned I'd get only eighty of it a week. That was for being a

Senior Writer, Junior Writers (midgets or minors, I guess) get seventy. A Senior Writer is expected to turn in fifteen hundred words of copy a day. The ideal item is a hundred words long, which means fifteen articles per diem per scriptorem maiorem. The point of having short articles is that, when published, the Revised Modern Universal International can claim that it has more entries than any other encyclopedia ever printed anywhere in any language at any time. When the editor hired me he explained that avowedly MUI would not be a work of original scholarship. At a considerable cost the company had gathered a large library of encyclopedias and other reference works, all of which were researched for relative reliability, so that, say, if Americana differed from Britannica on a death date of a seventeenth-century European, one or the other would be preferred. This library is the sole source for revising MUI. As a result, the editor said, we are in a precarious position. The day MUI comes out, every other encyclopedia on the market will begin going through it with (and I use his phrase) a fine-toothed comb. Now, although information is in the public domain, wording is not. Consequently one must rewrite. Rewrite, rewrite, rewrite. Any peculiar usage, no matter how attractive, must be avoided like (his words) the plague. Also—very, very important—the essential contents of every article done by a MUI writer must have appeared in at least two reference works in the MUI library. Encyclopedias, he said, have a way of using false entries—descriptions of non-existent machines, say, or biographies of non-existent people—so that when they show up in a new encyclopedia there is positive proof of plagiarism. Suppose, I said to the editor, one encyclopedia invents an entry for this purpose and then another encyclopedia steals it. There would be the two appearances necessary to get it into MUI. Ah, he said, obviously delighted at my immediate grasp of the larcenous possibilities of this business, we have made a study of plagiarism suits against reference works and we have excluded all cheaters from our library. Gee whiz, I said. So how did I get the job? Well, Harvey told me to forget about my stories—he had forgotten about his poetry—and clip out four so-called fictionalizations from movie magazines. Fictionalizations are anonymously written narratives, about five thousand words long, which describe in fulsome detail the plots of movies. Don't ask me why anyone would read a fictionalization rather than go to the movie, just take my word that such masochistic devices exist. Anyway, at Harvey's direction I went to a back-number magazine store, bought four old issues of a movie magazine, clipped out four fictionalizations, which Harvey checked to see that I wasn't using any he had used, assembled them in a leatherette folder to give the impression I was proud of them, and represented them as my own literary creation. The editor actually read one of them through, nodding here and there, and finally said I definitely had a sense of style. Anyway, my first week was a real piss. I just managed to rap out the fifteen hundred words a day, just managed. Then I'd go home and rewrite them in my head. I mean, I'd wake up in the middle of the night, and I'm not kidding, afraid that a phrase I'd used was too close to something in Webster's Bio or Columbia. But I was getting by, at least in the beginning. On the fourth day half the articles I had written on the first day were returned for stylistic improvement. Well, that day my new production was only five hundred words. The fifth day I got back two-thirds of the articles I had written on the second day. My new production was nothing. I came into the office an Saturday and Sunday, and somehow caught up. I should have pocketed my first week's salary and chucked the job there and then, but I just couldn't resist being a Writer. I mean, whenever I got talking to my new neighbors and they asked me what I did, I'd say I was a Writer, a Senior Writer for the Revised Modern Universal International, and they'd give me the large eye and the deferential nod. I was overcome with self-esteem. But what was I going to do? Well, my initial chat with the editor gave me an idea. Instead of fashioning inadequate compromises between this article in Larousse and that article in the D.A.B., I decided to invent. And what harm in this? No scholars would ever use MUI. MUI was interested in numerous entries and no plagiarism suits. What harm if I reported that William Abernathy, 1808–76, American abolitionist, minister, and author, had been born in Concord, Mass., of a long line of New England clerics? What harm that he had originally intended to enter business, but after the untimely death of his youngest son (1832), studied for the ministry, seeing in the tragedy a sign from God that he had erred in not taking up the work of his forebears? Or that his eloquence as a speaker made him highly revered, not only in Concord, but as far away as Boston, where he would be invited to address the congregations of different parishes on the spiritual and political concerns of the day? What harm? Or that an inner moral urging impelled him in later years to espouse the cause of Abolition, thus reversing a stand he had taken earlier in his life, when he had published the influential pamphlet Job Among Us, a closely reasoned argument that the Negro's suffering was a mark of God's special favor and that those who sought to abolish slavery were contradicting God's will? So Monday I returned to work and wrote twenty-seven hundred words. Tuesday three thousand, all while re-doing the previous week's work. Wednesday a terrible thing happened, the old stuff, after finally being passed for style, began returning from the checker. The checker! I thought this was all show biz, all illusion. Apparently not. Well, Friday the checker caught up with Monday. He came to see me personally. I confessed. Within an hour I was no longer a Writer. I tried to argue the editor into seeing these items as MUI's way of catching future plagiarists, but he had no imagination.

❈ ❈ ❈ ❈ ❈ ❈ ❈ ❈ WHY DIDN'T YOU tell me your mother was Jewish? With a Protestant father you must have had the same kind of deal I had. I'm not upset that you're such a sly one, I'm upset over the missed opportunities. A million times I could have said Some of my best friend is Jewish. Seriously, however, if I ever expressed any anti-semitic sentiments to you I want you to know that I meant every one of them. I didn't tell you, but Mary showed up at the funeral home. A right nice geste, I thought. I mean, she didn't know my father particularly. So we went out and had a drink afterward, and all the old thing came back. She is the third-most-beautiful girl I've ever seen. You know how I met her? In second-year high school I was the villain in the annual play, and between acts we all amused ourselves by peeking through the curtain and appraising the quiff in the audience. Up in a box was an assemblage of bright Irish-faced girls. Funny, I say that now, then that's all there was. If it wasn't a bright Irish-faced girl it was invisible. O there were sullen exotic Jewish girls, but one viewed them and was viewed by them with suspicion, and Protestant girls didn't seem interested or interesting. Fantasy directed you to the immaculate rosy mick, who you were sure ached as you did for carnal release. You just knew that she too lay abed at nights with the feminine equivalent of the implacable cock, seeking, seeking. She didn't, of course, but since girls never talked about themselves sexually you projected your own feelings into them, and you had the sense that she was locked, like yourself, against communicating the great need to anyone who could do something about it. Who knew then that girls are different creatures? Who knew that their tiny heads are full of flowers, dresses, silver service and a strong man standing by to kill spiders, make money, escort them to social functions, and occasionally in the darkness of the marriage bed kiss them on the cheek? Who knew then that just as the way to a man's heart is through his genital, the way to a woman's genital is through her heart? Don't tell me you did. All right, but if you did, it's because you were a Protestant Jew bastard. This is information they don't give out in Catholic grammar schools, where as far as the nuns are concerned, everyone, male or female, is dying to screw or at least play with himself. Grammar school was one long series of cautions. Keep your hands out of your pockets, don't linger in the bathtub, avoid dirty movies, dirty magazines, dirty books, dirty jokes and, most of all, provocative girls. Where the hell were the provocative girls, we all wanted to know. Anyway, I was peeking through the curtain, and there in the box, among the bright Irish faces, was a great bright Irish face. I see these great faces every now and then, in a bus, on the street, clerking in a department store. I've seen them all my life, but I never got to know one before. I mean, what are you going to do, walk up and say Miss, you have a great face? Well, it took me a half-hour to get the makeup off, but there in the lobby on the way out, being entertained in high style by an usher (a creepy guy who didn't get a part in the play) was the great face with her friends. The usher was big-dealing it as best he could from his ignoble station, and he called me over because I was an actor, put his arm around me and introduced me as if he was my proud father. Well, it turned out that the great face belonged to a senior in a local Catholic girls' school. Now, is there a longer distance than exists between a girl senior and a boy sophomore? Ah, but remember, I had been in the play, I had been the villain, and she accepted my invitation to go on the school boat ride. Since then I have anticipated parting other legs, grabbing other asses, but the month that separated that night from the day of the boat ride was the most expectant of my life. During the month I recalled only that she had a face you could swim in, and when I finally saw her again I was not disappointed. Tall and haughty with honey hair. Large round blue eyes and a perfect mouth, one of whose corners turned down and the other up when she smiled. And what a nose! It had a little bump from breaking it when she was a kid, which gave her that last touch of class. One of the guys on the boat ride asked me if she was my sister, and I nearly died with pride. Later I used to daydream about her really being my sister and me being in love with her nonetheless and crawling into her bed at night. So you can see, this was not a healthy relationship.

The rest you've heard, up and down, in and out. After a couple of years, when I discovered that her silences were not signs of deference to my wisdom but simple incomprehension, things became more difficult. But the great face remained, and the great face came to the funeral home. We've been out three times since then. Once we went to see a revival of La Dolce Vita, which I thought was tremendous and she thought was dirty. The second time I took her to an all-Mozart concert, which she said she liked but didn't. And the last time, which was two nights ago, we went to confession together. I mean, need I say more? Well, I will say more. A year or so ago I had reached the stage where if she'd listen to me I'd propose. It was like saying hello. Mary, dear heart, how have you been, will you marry me? I don't even know if I meant it. I'd ask, I think, with the idea that if she said yes, then I'd decide if I really wanted to. Not that there seemed to be much chance of that. I can only marry a Catholic, she'd say, a practicing Catholic. And you don't even try, you're not even interested, she'd add. How can I try, I'd ask, can I try to believe that peaches are blue? She didn't seem to get this. Say one Hail Mary every day, that's all I ask, just go through the motions, and grace will come. But I don't believe in grace, I don't believe in Hail Marys. Nonetheless, will you say the words? But I don't believe anybody's listening. At which she'd sigh a rattling sigh. All right, I'll say the words, I'll say the words. And she didn't understand me, I didn't want to be forgiven my sins or attain sanctifying grace or abide forever in the kingdom of heaven. The thought of never experiencing the presence of God did not fill me with a tragic sense of loss. All I wanted was to hold this beautiful Irish-faced girl in my arms. But I kept my promise. Hail Mary, full of grace! the Lord is with thee, blessed art thou among women, and blessed is the fruit of thy womb, Jesus. Holy Mary, Mother of God, pray for us sinners, now and at the hour of our death. Amen. And when I said it I thought that that Mary, whoever she is, wherever she is, is a bright Irish-faced girl like this Mary, perverted into religiosity by some crabbed rabbi. Hello Venus, full of juice! Cupid is with thee; blessed art thou among lovers, and blessed are the uses of thy womb, squeeze us. Sweetest Venus, Mother of Love, lay for us sinners, now and at the point of climax. Amen. That's my prayer. Anyway, she started it again at the funeral home and was at it every date since. If I go to confession, that will be making an honest effort, and she'd agree to be engaged. Suppose it doesn't work, I said. Suppose what doesn't work? Suppose I open my heart to grace and grace doesn't enter therein, what then? She'd be engaged to me anyhow, she said, because I tried. But there was about her smile when she said it a quality that meant such an eventuality was impossible. How could I open my heart to grace and grace not enter? God is ready with great syringes of grace, looking for the slightest aperture. Well, the last time I went to confession I had been fourteen. I was laying my hand on my gun and not telling it, and the rules of the game were that if you went to confession and withheld a mortal sin you were in effect lying and thereby committing another mortal sin.

So at fourteen I decided it was better to break the vicious circle and quit altogether. What a relief that was! I remember the day I made up my mind to chuck it. I was on my way to church, inventing sins to tell. Inventing them, like I cursed twice, Father, I was mean to my friend once, I took a dollar from my mother's purse, I committed the sin of pride by thinking I was smarter than everybody at a party, Father. Anything but the real thing. So I quit, and here I was now, ready to sink back into the whirlpool, begin again the endless alternation of sin and forgiveness. When the hell is it that you can live at peace with the Church? If you're not married, what do you do with your whacker, that tingles at every thigh emerging from a taxi, that as you crawl under the covers at night fills unprovoked with bloody blood, asking dumbly for shelter? And if you marry, if you do the bit, what then? They demand that you impregnate as you ejaculate. OK if you're rich, but suppose you're only a former writer at MUI? I figure the only way to be a good Catholic is to be rich, sterile, impotent, inhibitedly queer, or old. Old is best, old but with a wild sinful past, so there's no chance of senile where-did-it-all-go blues. Well, I'm none of these. Yet fixed by that great face I agreed to go to confession. Not on Saturday afternoon by myself, when I could sneak in one door and out the other. O no! Diabolically—or divinely, as you will—she had discovered a church that stayed open all night, ostensibly to service actors and such, but actually to catch the subtle change of mood, the lapse of sense in got-away Catholics. Like a twenty-four-hour cafeteria, the Church is ever ready with its ministrations, waiting for the suppressed guilt to rise and bring the sinner to his knees. And sure enough, there in the darkness of this ugly little church was a knot of penitents (from the Latin penis?) preparing themselves in pews that attended the brown-curtained box of forgiveness. When our turn came, Mary preceded me, and stayed but a minute or two. Bless me, Father, for I have sinned, I farted in public and caused others discomfort. My daughter, this is no sin, the others may offer up their discomfort for the suffering souls in purgatory. Well, she popped out and, head bowed, went to the altar to say her penance. I followed, down in darkness I went, onto a felt-covered kneeler, and began. Bless me, Father, for I have sinned. It has been seven years since my last good confession. In that time . . . , and I stopped. I hadn't given a thought to what I would say. Neither had I invented imaginary sins nor recollected real ones. And kneeling there I realized that if I ever intended to confess sincerely it would take enormous preparation. I had been away for seven years, not giving a damn—consciously anyway—and even when you're trying, really doing your best, it's a bitch to stay clean. You have to left-face, right-face, halt, march, double-time. Let me give you an example. When I was a kid, O twelve or thirteen, I had a compulsion to fashion naughty sayings from the call letters of radio stations. WEAF: Whores Enjoy All Fucking. Great witty truths like that, and each was a mortal sin. So what was I to say now? It was absurd. But this was an old story to the good all-night Father, I guess, because he helped out in my silence. Have you sinned against the sixth commandment, my son? I couldn't remember what the sixth was, but I had faith that like any Catholic cleric he had hit the trouble spot, so I said Yes, Father. Nor was I wrong. The sixth commandment, you Protesting Hebraic freethinker, is Thou shalt not commit adultery (or do any other dirty thing). He moved right in. Was this sin, or these sins, committed by yourself, with another person, or with an animal? So help me God, that is exactly what he said. By yourself, with another person, or with an animal. Well, two can play this game. All three, Father, I said. He wasn't fazed. Were the sins committed by yourself sins of thought, word, or deed? All, Father. How many times did you commit these sins? Many times, Father. Can you tell me how frequently? Quite frequently, Father. For seven years, he inquired. Yes, Father. How frequently did you commit the sin of deed by yourself? It varied, Father. Once a week, he asked. Yes, Father. More often? Sometimes, Father. Did you commit the sins of word and thought more often than the sins of deed? Yes, Father. How often have you committed sins with another person? Not as often, Father. (Which was putting it mildly.) Did you commit these sins with one person or more than one person? Do you mean at the same time, Father? No, serially. More than one person. Were the other persons of the same sex or the opposite sex. As myself you mean, Father? Yes. (Why should I discriminate, I thought.) Both, Father. Did you commit these sins more often with persons of the opposite sex or with persons of the same sex? (Here

I thought I'd draw the line.) Opposite, Father. And have you sinned with animals? (Jesus, what a dirty mind!) Yes, Father. Very often? No, Father. Have you committed mortal sins against any of the other commandments? Yes, Father. Which commandments? I was silent, I didn't know the goddamned numbers. But again he helped right out. Have you stolen? Yes, Father. A large amount? I paused, thinking of the complications, but what the hell! Yes, Father. More than a hundred dollars? Yes, Father. More than five hundred? Yes, Father. How much did you steal? Fifty thousand dollars, Father. Have you made restitution? No, Father. You must make restitution if you are to be forgiven, do you understand that? Yes, Father. Do you still have the money? Yes, Father. Do you intend to return it? Yes, Father. You must do this, if it is in your power. I understand, Father. Are you under suspicion for this crime? No, Father, I don't believe so. It is not necessary that you confess to the authorities, returning the stolen money is sufficient. Yes, Father, thank you. There was a mutual silence. I think he was afraid to go on. Finally, though, Have you committed any other serious sins? Yes, Father. Have you injured anyone? That isn't it, Father. You must tell me what it is, if you are to receive absolution. It's a very bad sin, Father. There is no sin beyond absolution if the sinner is repentant, what is the sin, my son? I'm ashamed to tell it, Father. You must, otherwise you cannot be absolved, do you understand that? Yes, Father, but I don't think this sin can be absolved. To believe that is a sin in itself, my son, God's mercy is infinitely large. Well then,

Father, I said, I have . . . lied in confession. And I broke out into nervous laughter, and I couldn't stop, so I beat it, nearly taking the curtain down as I went. Luckily Mary was waiting outside on the church steps. But talk about orgone boxes! The Pure Food and Drug people ought to get hot on confessionals, that's what I say. Anyway, she was suffused with happiness, certain that I must feel reborn. Quickly I got her away from the church, I was afraid somehow that the priest would come tailing after us. He didn't, of course. Did you say your penance, she asked. Well, I explained, the penance will take a little doing. She nodded understandingly, and we went off for a few drinks. Now we are engaged, really engaged, she said. But I had lost my taste for Mary. I took her home finally and kissed her lightly on the cheek and decided she was not for me.

❈ ❈ ❈ ❈ ❈ ❈ ❈ ❈ ❈ LAST NIGHT I fixed my own supper, two lamb chops and squash, and really that's not my dish, eating alone. There's nothing to slow you down. All the ritual that goes with company becomes pointless. Discreetly measure out vermouth and gin for the perfect martini, take your place at the table, sip martini, rise, put food on stove, artfully so that everything comes out simultaneously, sit down again, spread napkin on lap, cut meat with right hand, lay down knife, pick up fork, pop in morsel, chew politely with lips closed, wipe mouth, drink water, taste squash, jump up to turn off coffee, slice pecan ring, wrap up and put away, sit down, idle over coffee, rise again to find cigarette, take place, linger finally to savor the totality of the fine repast you have fashioned. Jesus, why not just slug the gin from the bottle, grab a few pieces of ham off the wax paper, another slug of gin, maybe a stalk of celery for the vitamins, and be about your business? Anyway, I did the bit, down to the place mat, faking full contentment. Maybe I even rubbed my stomach. And then I thought Ah, what shall I do for the evening? Go to a movie, a delicious piece of French sophistication? No, not quite. Perhaps stay home and read. What shall I read? Something old, something once read, something sure, to enjoy once again in my calm leisure. But it was fake, I didn't want to read, I didn't want to stay home. I wanted to fornicate, that's what I wanted to do. I wanted to get my duck wet and my heart wet. Here too my impulse was toward the sure thing. Toward Dorothy, but she was at summer school, having flunked most of her subjects in the spring term. Toward Judy, whom I could neck from the waist up, except that she had given me a hard time last time. She had pulled back and smiled and said Aren't you a hot little number! What a passionate little man you are! She closely escaped being smacked or raped that night. Maybe she wanted to be smacked or raped. But I wasn't in the smacking-raping mood, I was in the soft giving mood. Remember Roberta,

the one I took home from the party after her escort
passed out and she spread in the garage in her old man's
car? I could have, maybe I should have, looked her up.
But after that night I just let the thing dissolve. Now
why did I do that? Why didn't I keep it up? I mean, she
liked to screw. She wasn't bad looking, and why? I guess
because I didn't think she was screwing me, she was just
screwing. And could I call her up after all these months
and say Hi, Roberta, how the hell have you been? Girls
tend not to like that. O and I must explain that in the
next apartment a big party was waxing, twisting, cha-
cha-cha-ing, great loud laughings and someone banging
on the wall. It was the banging that finally got me. I
wanted to open the wall and say Come in, all you crazy
gay people, come in and enclose me. Vomit on my bed,
tear up my books, strew my closet's contents on the floor,
but do come in and enclose me, I'm lonely. Well, I've
been lonely more than once down here. Usually I knock
off half a pint of whatever's around, or maybe beer it up,
flop into the sack and wake up OK the next morn. But
this was worse than usual. I couldn't get into the goddamned bed, drunk or sober. Bed was where I became
loneliest. So I said to myself Be a man, comb your hair,
shine your shoes, get into that old Austin-Healey and
find yourself a girl. That's a cunt car. And man is a
hunter, is he not? Remember the time we picked up the
two Spanish girls in the spade bar? You bastard, slipping
in beside the skinny one and leaving me the two-ton bag.
What do you think about that big jigaboo, was he or
wasn't he pimping for them? You gentlemen don't mind

if Ah take these ladies with me, now, do you? Boy, did you give up quick! So, anyway, I got all slicked up, studied myself in the mirror and decided that I was good. Then I decided I was too good. I wanted a casual encounter. I couldn't go out like a high school kid full of hair oil and expect to catch a grownup thing. So I took off the tie and jacket, dashingly I rolled my shirt sleeves to the middle of the forearm, forced down a long one of gin and sauntered out to the old Austin-Healey. A teenage girl was sitting on the fender talking to another teenage girl. She jumped up when I put my hand on the door. I could see in their eyes So this is the guy that owns this groovy car. It was an auspicious start. The thought came and went that I should bow and say Girls, don't abuse your bums on this rust-spotted fender, settle them onto soft leather and I will take you for a whirlwind ride along the banks of yonder river. You know, I would have had a great time doing that, and afterward taking them to a drugstore and buying them sodas. It would have been a human encounter. But no, man, I was loaded and I was going. The town was mine tonight. A million chicks were out there waiting for me to cruise up in my unmufflered horizontal rocketship, a million tender-titted chicks, and I would pluck the chicest. I was full of gin, man, I was full of ennui dispelled. I could feel it, this was the beginning of a new life. No more Marys with their dry scruples, no more yearnings into domestic bedrooms wishing I were wed, with my own inexhaustible supply of ready pussy. No, man, I was going. Zoom, zoom! And I left the girls open-eyed as I pulled away, half depressing the clutch to sound the mighty motor loud and clear. Well, I drove, I drove up and down the streets and I saw everything. It was eleven o'clock when I started, and there were lovers and married couples and storekeepers locking up and guys hustling home from evening jobs and old men buying the morning papers and drunks and paired-up fags doing their stuff for the wide world to see, all the time making like there was no world about them. Jesus, a great black bug just crawled over the rug. Big as a toy. I hit it with the typewriter case, and it's mashed there. Wait a minute, I'm going back and cover it up. Jesus, an animal! Anyway, there were girls too, in groups and alone. Yet what was I supposed to do? Pull over to the curb, honk my horn and wink? The more I drove and the more girls I saw, the more I realized I just couldn't in effect say My dear, the tension in this groin has reached unbearable proportions, how would you like to listen to some inept sweet talk for an hour so that I can relieve myself? Of course, I would expect you to ignore the fact that I might be taking your maidenhead, which you'd like to save for the man you marry, ignore the fact that I might knock you up, in which case you could count on me for a suspicious donation toward an abortion, during which you might die. I would expect you to forget these and other possibilities and commit yourself to the spirit of the moment. And yet guys do this, do this every day and night, and make out. If they didn't make out, would I see them by the hundreds, these conscienceless hunters in their bright sports shirts and sports convertibles? I saw college kids too, or college-type kids, pushing each other around on sidewalks, or walking and talking in pairs heatedly, about what? What did we talk about? I almost forget. I wasn't of them any more. I didn't belong to an institution that demanded things of me as the price of belonging, I didn't even belong to a family, to a shitty burdensome family. I was free, to be nothing. Has this happened to you yet? Is it just me, or what? Only once before in my life was I so low. When I was a kid, thirteen or thereabouts, my skin broke out and I didn't go to a beach party I was supposed to, I just stayed home in the dark, lying on a glider on a screened-in porch at the summer place. My mother was with neighbors, and my father was off night-fishing. I remember touching my face with the pads of my fingers, crying lightly till there was no more liquid in my cryballs. It wasn't just the beginning of adolescence. That summer night and this summer night in my Austin-Healey I was in touch with the truth about the so-called human condition. It ain't so good, brother. I mean, give me the razzmatazz, give me the noise. I don't need these moments of truth at all at all. Well, I kept going, driving up and down streets, fast and slow, passing red lights, stopping for green, and then I had an idea. I would go to the beach. It would take me an hour to get there, but at least then I could clean myself in the cool water. It was a lonely drive, the way I went, and I kept sinking down. I hit absolute zero, and when I got there I couldn't even take my clothes off. I stumbled down the long shore and went into the water with them on. Even that didn't help. I stood there with the little waves whacking at my belt.

I thought of my father and how I had never had one really spontaneous moment with him. I thought of my old lady stiff-lipping it with her brother. Beautiful Mary with the great face, soon to be dehumanized by Catholicism. And I thought of myself, standing in the ocean like a nut, asking God, whom I didn't believe in, to do something for me. I said Dear Jesus, fix whatever is wrong with me or the world. But the words didn't rise, they hovered in the air and slipped into the water. I got back into the car and drove home. Man, had I gotten my duck wet! It was four o'clock when I went to bed. If I hadn't fallen asleep I don't know what would have happened. But I did and I dreamed. A girl at the encyclopedia—a real girl, except that I never knew her to speak to—came up to me and put her head on my shoulder and cried. I asked her what the matter was, and she said she laid for people she didn't like. I said I did too and it wasn't such a terrible thing, and she said that for a man it was different. I asked her if she liked me. She said yes, and we made love. I woke up about noon today and felt great. Now what the hell does all that mean?

❈ ❈ ❈ ❈ ❈ ❈ ❈ ❈ ❈ NOW GET THIS. I was on the can this afternoon, taking my time, thinking nothing, when I looked down, and my hands were gone. My shirt sleeves were there, but nothing came out of the cuffs. I dropped my hands, or what felt like my hands, from my lap and stared straight ahead at the bathroom door. My first thought was that I might have died without knowing it. But then I reasoned that it might be a momentary optical trick like a dizzy spell or spots before my eyes. I decided to find out if my sense of touch was normal. I closed my eyes to avoid the original shock again, I closed my eyes but I continued seeing everything, the door, the sink, the ceiling. Now with my eyelids drawn down but my vision unblocked, it took all my will power to keep from panic. I didn't know what to do. I just kept my head pushed forward and upward, and my hands hanging down, so I wouldn't see exposed portions of my body again. Then I realized that in the periphery of my vision there was no sign of eyebrows, eyelashes or nose. It was as if my eyeballs were propped out on sticks. Carefully I leaned forward so I could reach my feet with my hands. I squeezed my shoes, patted my ankles, and slowly worked up. Everything seemed to be there. Finally I gathered enough courage to look at my hands again, I raised them in front of my face. Empty cuffs! I peered into the cuffs. The cloth was drawn tight at the elbows. I pressed my hands against my face. They were warm and damp, but they didn't shut off my vision. I was scared. I pushed my pants from my thighs and looked down through the hollow legs at the dark insides of my shoes. I couldn't see even an outline of flesh. I ripped the buttons off my shirt and yanked up the undershirt. It bunched on my chest over nothing that I could see. Then I panicked. No one must see me like this, so I hauled up shorts and pants, tucked in my undershirt, and turned around to look in the mirror. Like a shot I sat down again. In the mirror it seemed as if my head was cut off. Now there were two possibilities, both as far as what had happened to me and what to do about it. Either this was an illusion, in which case I was sick; or else it was a fact, in which case other people couldn't see me either. Which it was would be easy enough to find out. All I had to do was walk into the hall with my clothes on and wait for someone to come along. If that someone was dumfounded at the headless figure, then it was an objective fact. The alternative test would be to take off all my clothes before going out. Then, if it was an illusion, I'd be taken to a hospital for exposing myself. There didn't seem to be any question about which test to choose. I'd go out naked, and if it wasn't all my imagination, at least I'd have a chance to decide for myself how to operate. Otherwise I'd end up in some scientific laboratory, and the fact that I was a human being and a citizen wouldn't count for a thing. I could see it. With clothes on, I'd manage to get out of the building, but once on the streets crowds would gather and surge around me. At first no one would touch the headless figure, they'd be too frightened. But finally the police would come because of the commotion and take me into custody. I would have committed no crime, but I would be a prisoner. Newspapers would unpack their war-size headlines to announce the incredible phenomenon. Reporters would demand to see me, they'd want pictures for their doubting readers. The authorities would have to give in. A press conference would be arranged, to which not only newsmen but representatives of all the communication media of all the countries in the world would show up. And at this point I'd make a magnificent speech. Science be damned, I'd say. I'm a human being and a citizen of the United States and I'm being held against my will without due process of law. I'd work into an eloquent passage about the meaning of individual rights, the pursuit of happiness and all that. The papers would eat it up. The whole world would read about me, first in wonderment and then in sympathy. Editorials would be written, demands made by freedom-loving citizens' groups, for my release. But the scientists would fight to hold me. The case would be argued in every quarter of the land, and finally in the Supreme Court itself, where a history-making decision would be delivered re-establishing the prerogatives of the common man. New meaning would have been given to the Constitution, and after the dust settled I would retire into private life on a government grant, so that I could not become a victim of commercial exploitation. Then and only then might I possibly co-operate with the scientists. But a cold thought broke into my reverie. It was much more probable that I was sick and that this was the beginning of many years inside a mental institution, where I would undergo shock treatments and suffer untold interior self-made agonies. Now I became certain that it was a trick of the mind, and rejected the idea of undressing and going out into the hall. Somehow I would get down to my car in front of the house, close the top and drive to my mother's place. She would call the doctor, and maybe I could be treated privately instead of in an institution. I couldn't make up my mind. I looked at my hands again to see if they would answer the problem for me. I moved them about, rubbed one on the other, looking for an outline or hint of flesh. None. I began to study the insides of the cuffs. If this was all an illusion, it certainly was perfect. Not only couldn't I see my hands, but my mind was inventing the parts of the cuffs that should have been hidden by my wrists. I could see how every fiber was woven into every other, I could even see the tiny imperfections in the cloth. Then I suddenly became aware of almost imperceptible fragments of dirt under my fingernails. The difficulty in seeing them before, I understood, lay not so much in that they were slight but in that the eye had no guide to help focus on them. I tore off a piece of toilet tissue, put it on my knee and my hand on top of the tissue to provide a white background. Now I could see the fingernail dirt plainly and just barely make out the form of a hand from the bits of foreign matter that adhered to the skin. It was only the tenderest ghost, but it was infinitely better than nothing. I bent over and rubbed the pad of my index finger on the tile floor. I held the finger up. A semi-opaque spot. When I turned the finger sideways, the spot became a delicate cup hanging in air. Then I drew my whole palm along the floor. A floating handprint. If I looked closely I could even see the grain of skin. It reminded me of a trick of my childhood, putting a coin under a piece of paper and rubbing a pencil on top of it to get a picture of the coin.

The handprint gave me courage. I decided to go out into the hall naked. So what do you think, man? That's the beginning of my novel. I've been sitting around here day after day wasting my patrimony, or should I say matrimony, and I decided to take the plunge. Am I not onto something? Let me ask you. When you started reading, did you think I had flipped my lid? Did you know it was an entertainment? You see, what I'm going to do is send the poor slob out into the hall naked to wait for his first encounter, let's say a girl walking slowly up the stairs. Will she scream, or just walk by unseeing? She walks by, he's overjoyed. It means that he isn't sick, that he's really invisible, and out of sheer exuberance he slips her a mighty goose. But once on the street he has difficulties. For one thing, in the sun his eyes burn because he can't shade them. And the dirt of the sidewalk sticks to his feet. He has a hell of a time getting food and has to hide when he eats because it takes about half an hour for him to digest. Contrariwise he pees in the gutter and watches the pee slowly materialize before his eyes as it ceases to be a part of him. Now, the book will concern the contrast between his actual situation, which is desperate because he's afraid of being captured by the scientists, and his ambition to take full advantage of his condition, rule the world by influencing national leaders, discover the secrets of history by being privy to the conversations of powerful people, lay the world's most beautiful women by moving in on them in the darkness of the night. I have to figure out a gimmick to account for his invisibility—which word, by the way, I'm not going to mention in the book—and since the thing happens to him on the can I'm considering using what I call the floggis, a semi-substantial organ common to all living things, which this poor bugger shakes loose from its moorings and defecates. At the end of the book he'll find it somewhere, swallow it and become opaque again. You like?

ℵ ℵ ℵ ℵ ℵ ℵ ℵ ℵ ℵ LIFE, SAYS THE philosopher, is a succession of compensations—if you're lucky. I'm lucky. I lose my job, but I begin a novel. My novel stops, but I get another job. I don't like the job, but I meet the girl of my dreams. I am no longer a Writer, but I become a legend. Twenty-one and already a legend. It seems that after I left MUI, word of my little biographical inventions spread. The articles were copied on a photo machine and circulated among the help. Staffers who never paid me any heed while I was there began to talk about me. Harvey, the protean faker and fucker, took full advantage of this posthumous fame to get me the other job. He himself had been promoted to chief caption writer at a hundred-and-twenty a week, which both delights and surprises me. I mean, remember what an undisciplined slob he seemed to be at school? With MUI, at least according to Harvey, he is a respected craftsman, a judge of literary style, a master of concision and clarity, a graphic aesthetician. The publisher himself comes to Harvey with the subtlest problems, choices of type face, for instance, and Harvey delivers judgments. He claims he knows nothing of these matters—which claim I have no reason to doubt—but he makes strong arbitrary decisions, backing them up with abstract double talk, and people defer. Harvey says that everybody else at MUI knows a little and consequently is uncertain, whereas he knows nothing and has no doubts. As for caption-writing, which is supposed to demand a special talent, Harvey explains that he merely names the contents of the pictures with the shortest words he knows, arranging them in subject-verb-object order, denies every impulse to use colons and semicolons, and has gained thereby a reputation for expository genius. Anyway, the art department, which was made up of Harvey and the lady art director, decided it needed a picture editor. That's me. It sounds better than it is, actually. I just hustle my ass around and gather up as many free pictures as I can, from industrial associations, museums, libraries, publicity agents, vacant lots, burned warehouses, garbage cans, and since MUI is an A-to-Z encyclopedia everything theoretically comes in handy. The editor didn't like the idea of hiring me back, but the art director convinced him that I couldn't cheat with pictures. I haven't tried yet, we'll have to see. When she interviewed me and I told her I didn't know anything about pictures, she said Don't worry, you'll learn, and she showed me a few pairs of photographs. Pick the better ones, she said. In each case I chose the clearer, and this really astounded her. Perfect, she said, perfect! She got all excited, which made me feel like Harvey with his captions. Then, after she hired me, she asked me to tell her the details of getting fired from the writing job. She couldn't control herself, every time I mentioned the editor's name, she slapped her knees in delight. My first day back, four people came up to me, introduced themselves, and asked for the same story. The second day back, the publisher himself, a speedy little character named Harry Fox, called me to his office, ostensibly to look over the new picture editor, but really to hear the story. From his amusement I guessed he didn't like the editor either. As who can blame him? The editor is a big pompous jerk who keeps his jacket on and is said to be banging his secretary, a pimply stringy-haired girl without eyeteeth. MUI's office is a former town house, very elegant. The writers work in the ballroom, to give you an idea. The art department was once the music room, there's still a pipe organ against the far wall. The top floor has been made over into an apartment for the publisher and his guests. He doesn't live there, just flops after the opera, or so he says. I understand he doesn't flop alone, however. Nor is he the only one that doesn't flop alone up there. So let me tell you. This was before I went back. Harvey was working late one night, expunging adjectives from his captions, when who should wander into the music room but Mrs. Fox, wife to the publisher. I've never seen her, but according to Harvey she's a well-preserved, ample-breasted, small-waisted, thick-calved, purple-tinted, seasonally tanned grandma of forty-five.

Also a crazy good screw, Harvey says. Do you work for my husband, she asks, immediately defining the relationship, because I have a dreadful throat. Would you be a wonderful man and run down to the drugstore and get me some orange juice? I'd go myself, but I'm expecting an important call from Mr. Fox, and so on. Well, old Harvey told her he didn't think orange juice was any good for a sore throat, but he'd be glad to take her out for a drink if she could wait fifteen minutes until he finished what he was doing. I knew the instant I saw her nosing around, Harvey said, that she was looking for a mount from the stable. The question was who was going to be on top, the proprietor's lady or the hired help. Well, whoever ended on top, they seemed to have developed quite an affection for one another, because they've used the upstairs apartment every night for two weeks, Harvey running home to change his shirt once in a while and explaining to his parents that he's collaborating with a composer on a musical comedy. Well, as Harvey continued to leave off-white badges of honor on the publisher's sheets he wondered how come Mr. Fox wasn't more concerned about Mrs. Fox's whereabouts of nights, how come in fact he wasn't using the apartment himself. The question was solved one afternoon when Fox called Harvey to his office. It's a great Persian-rugged affair with a genuine stained-glass window. I understand, Fox says, bang, that you are in love with my wife and that my wife is in love with you, is this true? Well, Harvey sort of mumbles and nods to keep from fainting. I want you to understand my position, Fox says, I have no intention of standing in your way. I've had too many happy years with Mrs. Fox not to respect her emotional needs. I deeply respect the fact that she came to me honestly and openly and told me what happened. I value her for this. I would like you to be just as straightforward. Well, Harvey said that at first he was just too embarrassed to tell the publisher the truth, which was that he was only having a ball for himself. After all, this was the man's wife, it would have been impolite. So he just sort of praised him for his generosity and compassion, but did he want to get out of there! Well, Fox keeps pushing this broadminded line until finally Harvey has to tell him that he doesn't think his parents would approve of a formal liaison like marriage. Because of the difference in ages, Harvey explained. Whereat Fox apparently concluded that he was dealing with a businessman, because he pours Harvey a glass of man-to-man Scotch and begins to level. It seems that he also is in love with another party—a young lady just about Harvey's age. O everything he had said about desiring his wife's happiness is true, but there are other factors. He would much prefer that Mrs. Fox initiate the divorce proceedings. Not only would she be unhurt that way, but the backing for MUI is coming from her brother, who definitely would not be unhurt if he thought Fox was deserting his sister after all these years. O yes, Mrs. Fox belongs to a very wealthy family, and the publisher ticks off some of her holdings. Also he explains that it is not unusual in these cases for a premarital settlement to be made on the husband, as in fact it had been made on him when he married her, in exchange for signing away all rights to the estate. Why, such a settlement, Fox said, might amount to a hundred thousand dollars, and Harvey should understand that the money would be free and clear, regardless of the progress of the marriage. You mean I could dump her afterward, Harvey said. Exactly, the publisher said. I also thought that a quiet wedding gift from me to you might make the move easier. Say, ten thousand dollars. Well, everybody's cards were on the desk, and Harvey told Fox he needed time to think it over. Now let me contrast these crass dealings with my own romantic adventures. One of the people who came to see me the day I got back was the girl I dreamed about, the one who put her head on my shoulder and cried. I was actually embarrassed. I mean, we had made love in the dream, which she knew nothing about, of course, but there she was, standing next to my desk, and I was suffused with groiny, comey pleasure. In her hand she had a copy of one of my biographies, about Evan Price, a Salem witch-burner, who had proposed the theory that the local female weirdies were not only possessed of Satan but had regular carnal conversation with him too. Price's claim to fame rested on the historical fact that he caused three infants, who were supposed to have been sired by the devil, to be burned at small stakes. I had put it all in good encyclopedic language, but nonetheless she thought it was a poignant story. I said I had intended it to be kind of funny, and she said it was, in a poignant way. Well, her name is Prudence, which she says her parents gave her because they waited five years to have her and even then she was a ten-month baby. If her face was made of anything but flesh it would be pretty plain, but she has this fantastic skin, golden and downy with an oval of deep pink on each cheek. I think a drop of water would roll over her skin like mercury. In fact, when she cried in my dream the tears did sort of slide without sinking in. I want to apologize for that letter, by the way. You once said you didn't like people dumping their souls in your lap, but, Jesus, I felt bad. I guess it was a combination of my father dying and being on my own suddenly. I don't think it will happen again, and I think that Prudence is the reason why it won't. There's a kind of sad solidity about her that makes her very valuable to me. I don't even know for what, but as if in her there is an important answer for me about myself. Well, anyway, we had lunch together a couple of times, and when I wanted her to see a movie or something with me after work, she asked me to come to her home for dinner instead. To say it was a nice home won't do it, to say that it was posh or impressive won't do it. It was all this, but it was also the most attractive home I've ever been in. It's about twenty miles above the city line, along the river. You can't see it from the road. The path from the road winds in among trees, and suddenly you come on what looks like a magic cottage. But this is only the front. Behind, the house gets bigger and goes down. It's built on a slope that falls to the river, and instead of the floors being piled one on top of the other, they accumulate gradually one under the other. In the back is a large garden with a gazebo and stone seats and finally a dock.

They turned the lights on for me, the air was wet and still and held the bitter smell of leaves and grass. It was like a fairyland. But after dinner, before it got dark, Prudence, her younger sister Billy, and I sat on a stone bench and said almost nothing for I guess an hour, we just listened to the lips of waves talking to the rocks and pilings. I haven't seen it in full daylight yet, but given a bright afternoon I could imagine never wanting to leave that garden. For a city boy, this was something. No, not for a city boy, I've been to expensive country homes, but most of them do nothing for me, no style, just an arrangement imposed on the ground. But Prudence's home has that deepness that comes to things used by people with good hearts. I sound like I'm in love. Well, if I am, it's not with Prudence only or her home. It's with Prudence and her home and her family. The three of them, her sister Billy, who I guess is about fourteen, and Mommie, who, considering that she waited five years to have Prudence, looks as if she must have married at ten. All of them have this wild skin, the golden hue with pink ovals. I never saw anything like it. It's as if they were three inspired dolls. The old man is dead. They didn't talk much about him, he died from cancer five years ago, but they all seem to revolve about his absence. Prudence showed me his picture, and he looked like a nice man. Nice in the way people you know are dead look nice, but also nice like he had realized his manhood not at anybody else's expense. I knew from the minute I pulled into the driveway that Prudence had honored me by asking me there, but it wasn't until she showed me the picture that I understood how much. At dinner I was it. I mean, the three of them seemed to feed off my manness, and their need brought manness out in me. I wanted to give of myself to all of them, each in the way she desired. And I did. I was capable of being a contemporary to Billy, Prudence, and Mommie together. Playmate and boyfriend and daddie and son and husband. How about that?

✻ ✻ ✻ ✻ ✻ ✻ ✻ ✻ IT'S REALLY TOO late to be writing. In fact I'm afraid if I look at the clock I'll fall asleep. But I had to tell you that there was a guy in here tonight, he lives in this building, on my floor, who flipped for the novel. But first let me tell you what happened this afternoon. The lady art director made out a list of free pictures to get from the public library, illustrations for Gemini, General Grant National Park, generator, Genesis, Geneva, Genghis Khan, genitalia, and Genoa. Photographs of General Grant National Park, Geneva, and Genoa, she said. Diagram of a simple generator. An old Bible history picture for Genesis. Something similar for Gemini. All in the public domain, mind you. Check the copyright. O yes, and something stylized for genitalia. You know, she said, stylized. Sure, I said, but I didn't really. I mean, I did know and I didn't know, if you know what I mean. Anyway, the library's picture collection is a big junkyard of folders arranged alphabetically under some pretty strange titles. If you know where to look you can get a picture of almost anything. Like genitalia might be under reproductive system, or crotch, or fun & games. Anyway, I rounded up everything but the stylized you know what, and I had tried all the possibilities, including cock and cunt. Well, finally I hitched up my moxie and told the ancient maiden-in-charge about my genitalia problem. And she did nothing to put me at my ease. In fact she opened her watery blue eyes a little wider as if to let me know that she had had experience with perverts like me before. Then she called from her office a rosy little chicken about seventeen and told her to get the, and she paused, the atlas. The girl glanced at me nervously and went off to obey. The, ahem, atlas was a book about a yard big both ways. You will find here, old bitch said, in this anatomical atlas, pictures of every part of the human body. It is a very valuable book, please handle it with care. Then discreetly she took the young girl aside. It was fascinating, the most detailed etchings I have ever seen of anything. On the left, say, would be a male arm and hand, the fingers curling up in a kind of absolute relaxation. On the right, a woman's arm and hand. And so on, page after page. It reminded me of those juxta-linear translations, Latin on one side, English on the other. Limbs were severed from the body proper, and even the exposed veins and muscles were represented with exquisite accuracy. What was so interesting and uneasy-making, though, was that the pictures lacked comment, as if they had been etched by a machine rather than an artist. So I looked at the title page, and might have known, published Leipzig 1882. Well, I worked my way, turning the newspaper-size pages, through feet and calves and tits and butts and two rather beautiful heads, which in their innocence looked like Adam and Eve, on to the pookies. On the left the male organ lay against a thigh like a sleeping bird. And on the right, ladies and gentlemen, was the cause of all male joy and sorrow, the much-storied fountain of youth, the rancid sump seen by Church Fathers, the fur-lined honeytub of adolescent boys, the saw-toothed monster of frightened fags, the perfumed rose of healthy dreams. In a word, vagina beatissima. I nodded toward the two females, who had been waiting like salesladies. May I borrow this to have it copied, I asked in my most picture-editor manner. We don't lend bound books from this department, bitch said, only loose pictures. You may have it photostatted in the library, however. All right, I said, and went to pick the book up, at which bitch propelled her tender helper toward me. The girl took the great open book like a tray from my hands. Let me help, I said. She turned away, refusing my offer, and we marched, I behind, she before, out of the picture collection, down the hall, into the elevator, she just barely maintaining the thing on her hands and forearms. The poor baby's high color heightened further in transit, and in the elevator everyone had a look, at me, at her, at the open book. It was as if I hadn't shut the bathroom door. The photostat department was also manned by a woman. We put the book on her counter, and I told her my desires. You must pay in advance, she said. I did, and will you send me the stats? Disdainfully she told me that these pictures could not be sent through the mails. All right, I said, completely shamed by now, I'll pick them up on my next trip. And as I turned to leave I saw her close the book, bringing the facing pages together with distaste. Back at MUI, the art director said that in my absence she had found exactly what was needed in the American Health Encyclopedia. She showed me the pictures, and I understood what she had meant by stylized, an arrow and a circle, for Chrissake. Anyway, the guy who read the novel is a handsome, drooping-mustachioed young Spaniard named Jose Llano. His family name means both plane and plain, he told me. Very appropriate, he said, for I am a flat and ordinary fellow. Flat he is, skinnier than I am, but ordinary he's not. For instance, he has a wild attitude toward copulation, he's against it. He practices it, but he's against it. No escape, he says, you walk through the fields, ravished by the flowers, plucking, plucking, until one day a flower plucks you. You marry, you fertilize, you rear, you're through. It will happen to you, he says, yes, it will even happen to me. Then I shall forget my music and mathematics, resign myself to translating for a bank doing business with South America, retire at sixty-five, and die at sixty-six. Coitus, he said, and spat without spittle. Degrading, and he spat again. Coitus is for weekdays. But masturbation, masturbation is for Sunday. With masturbation you slap nature in the face, trample the grave of Darwin, distinguish yourself from the animals. I can't tell if he's serious or not, but I know he's fantastically smart. Harvey claims he's the only authentic genius he's ever met. I got to know him in a peculiar way. He had heard that I was a writer for MUI and came to ask my help with the spelling in a children's book he's writing. It's called Very Tales and is intended to explain to kids, through little didactic stories, the true nature of the universe. For instance, he showed me his Very Tale about relativity. This is how it goes after I cleaned up the English. Once upon a time there was a man who had a pimple in the middle of his back. Try as he might he could not reach it, and the pimple grew bigger and bigger. So big, in fact, that it became a question whether the man had the pimple or the pimple had the man. Whichever was the case, the two of them were out walking one day when they happened to meet a pure pimple, that is, an unattached pimple, which was, from a pimplish point of view, a very handsome pimple. Red and shiny and taut with a great white head like an albino volcano. The handsome pimple, seeing the other pimple so badly blemished by the rough hairy man, said You should really do something about yourself, my dear. You could be a very attractive pimple if you only took care of your complexion. Whereat the pimple with the man began to cry. Don't worry, don't worry, the handsome pimple said, I'll take you to my dermatologist, and in no time you'll be on your way to beauty and happiness. And that very day the handsome pimple took the blemished pimple to the doctor. The doctor shook his

head and clicked his tongue and said that in his entire
career he had never seen anything like it. But I think we
can help you, he said, whereupon he put the pimple up
on a leather table, removed the scraps of clothing that
adhered to the man, and with the help of a nurse
squeezed the man until he burst. O what a relief for the
pimple! Now, keep this bandage on for a week, the doctor said, and don't worry about a thing. You're going to
be all right. And sure enough, after a week, when the
bandage came off, only the tiniest scar remained where
the man had been. I took it to work and showed it to
Prudence, she said it made her sick. I showed it to the
art director. She accused me of writing it, saying it reminded her of my biographical articles for MUI. Harvey
said it was genuine dada prose and high art. He also said
it would make a great movie. I mentioned this to Jose,
and now he's trying to get Harvey to collaborate with
him on a scenario. Anyway, tonight, more to reciprocate
than get help I gave the beginning of the novel to Jose.
He took it, not reluctantly so much as with a touch of
contempt, like it was all right for me to help him out
with the mechanics of English but I shouldn't presume to swap fiction with him. Nonetheless he was back
in half an hour saying that I was on the verge of creating
another Don Quixote.

✖ ✖ ✖ ✖ ✖ ✖ ✖ ✖ ✖ ✖ I WAS DOWN shining up the car yesterday, Saturday morning, and three old ladies came along, one in a wheel chair, two pushing. Old, old ladies, and I was feeling great and I said Enjoy the day, ladies. They smiled, they looked at each other, they thanked me and they wished me the same, and as they pushed away they turned around and I knew they were talking about me. They were saying What a nice boy, does he live around here? And they liked me, they liked what I had said, because people don't dig old ladies very much or often. People steer clear, look askance, try to forget old ladies. And old ladies know this. But I had said Enjoy the day, ladies, because as soon as I saw them I knew that, an hour before, they had looked from their windows and seen the beauty of the day and wondered whether to go abroad, whether to hoist one of themselves into the wheel chair, work it onto the elevator, down the front steps. A large question, this going to the river, or just to the corner and back, a question equal in their youth to going away for the weekend. Shall we submit to the fuss, the packing and unpacking, dare we chance the car (I don't like that rear tire, Frank said we ought to get a new one, and I should have, but I've kept postponing, and the garage is probably closed now), and they were nice-looking old ladies. What I mean is they seemed to know the woman business. Years before, they were made much of, I could tell, by girlfriends who were jealous, by parents eager that they have dignity and self-esteem, by young men trying to make out and in. And nobody wants anything of them any more except their absence, no daddies want to be adored by them, no mommies want them to become what they were not, no boyfriends dream of final contentment in their coozies, no merchants fawn for their gold and expected gold. All these attentions were long ago. Now one is riding, two are walking. Soon one of them will be gone, and another will ride, with only the third left to push, slowly, fearful of the curbs, and I had said Enjoy the day, ladies. And I was young, I could have been ten or fifteen as well as twenty-one, so distant was I from them. How did I know enough to tell them to enjoy the day? How did I know, being what they were once and weren't any more? I mean, the fresh sweat was dripping inside my T shirt, my hair was matted, my muscles ached. I was taking the car's dirt onto myself, and in a little while I would commend that dirt to the shower drain, and then both of us, the car and I, would be clean to ride the second law of thermodynamics, spreading our heats through the universe. We have great heats in us, the car and I, high caloric potentials, great descents from heat to cold, while these old ladies emit small resources cautiously. This warm clear day was undemanding, would not draw unduly on their diminished stores. So they chanced it, put their bodies to the expedition in order that their minds might experience the world again, not the world of room and bed, but the world of ragged kids and pregnant women and ice-cream men and frowning cops and dark shoulders hunched in darker windows. How to spend these daily pieces of the remaining month, year, decade? Yesterday they opted for life, bought a few minutes of the earth with a nickel of their fund, and I had said Enjoy the day, ladies. We understood each other, the old ladies and I. In a little while they came back, smiling as they came. I put down the Simonize and smiled. You must have a girl, the one in the wheel chair said. Yes, I said, I do. And she looked to the others for credit. I must have a girl, and I thought after they had gone, this is how old ladies see it. Boys have girls, girls are had by boys. From these old ladies childhood admonitions about and against sex had dropped away. It no longer seemed to them a problem to be female, you choose a man, he chooses you, he has his way with you, but you with him, he works, you bear, you both donate your bodies to the future and you die. Why do the young females make such a thing of it, the old ladies think now. Here is this nice boy, who only means them well, and they whirl, whirl, whirl. Lie still, young girl, commit yourself to, what, yourself. You know, I'm wondering if life really is as hard as they say. At Jose's behest I read a book by Unamuno, The Tragic Sense of Life, which showed how all great philosophic inventions are merely artful attempts to prove one or another kind of immortality, that it is a universal human hope to live forever. I don't feel it. I mean, I don't want to die today, or tomorrow, but let the body wear out and I'll go. We had this argument once before, didn't we? You said I'd feel differently when the time came, that then I'd ask for a little more, and then a little more, and finally go out screaming. Well, maybe. I mean, who knows? But if I plant seeds now, and my garden grows, why won't I be willing to leave off? If the seeds don't grow, ah that's another matter. But why shouldn't they grow? I'm not asking for redwoods. I'll tell you what I mean. I was shining the car because I was going up to Prudence's for dinner. She likes to stay in the country on weekends, we thought we'd miss each other, and since her mother was doing a dinner for a friend of her own, why not? So I drove up. Once you get out of the city the highway works between trees, goes up and down and around curves, the river breaks into sight and disappears. Only the true comprehenders of entropy appreciate this road, we transformers of cold air into hot breath, we tilters of axles, sounders of horns. Well, Mamma's friend turned out to be a pudgy, balding lay-priest type, bright baby eyes and ever-ready chuckles. I disliked him right off and looked to Prudence and Billy—not to Mamma because he was, after all, her friend—for signs of repulsion. But they liked the guy, listened to his stories—he was a great traveler—ohing and ahing him at every stop. Then halfway through the meal I decided Who was I? This wasn't my party, it was Mamma's party, and she enjoyed the guy, so sit back and relax. Not everybody has to be made for my delight to be worthy of existence. And I did, I sat back, the guy liked to talk, and with the others I listened and I enjoyed. I think I had disliked the guy because I wanted Mamma to have herself a friend more like the dead daddy. But maybe she had had the dead daddy, maybe she just wanted something moderate, a male of sorts, gentle and articulate, and no more. So settle down, I told myself. There was another aspect. Secretly I had hoped that Prudence and her mother would ask me to stay the night. O it's such a long trip back to town, and it's so late now, why don't you? And secretly secretly I had hoped that deep in the darkness of the early morning my unsqueaking door would open and Prudence would come in. Funny, I want to go to bed with Prudence and I don't have to. There's something very tender about her, which I must not injure, a tenderness in her and a tenderness in me about her tenderness, and properly worked together I think they will make a third very strong thing. Well, anyway, Mr. Pudgybald had come up by train, and it was arranged before I arrived that he would drive back with me. Boy! But, as I said, it went well, once I relaxed. I had the same feeling I had the first time I visited Prudence, a sense that I was getting through as an equal. In my own family, my mother always listened and agreed, but it didn't mean anything, she agreed with everything. And my father agreed with nothing. Every response he made was intended to shift my opinions in a useful direction. As an instance, if I had asked him whether he believed in free will, he wouldn't tell me his own feelings, he'd say what was calculated to be for my best interest. I never actually asked my father about free will, but it occurs to me now because I did once ask Professor Duffy about it. He was also interested in my well-being, but I guess he thought it would be best served by telling me what he really thought. He said that when he was young he had put just this question to a particularly wise friend, and the friend had said it was an unanswerable question, but one thing was sure, if man does have free will he can lose it by not believing in it. A kind of Pascal's Wager, only practical. Now, that was an answer, and I went away believing in free will. O I guess I shouldn't disparage my old man, he did his best by me and everybody. But what I mean is that neither time at Prudence's house did I or Prudence or Billy or Mamma fake. We practiced discretion and all, but we could speak our minds without fear of disapproval or correction. Each of us was interested in the others as they were. Billy with her big eyes and crooked bottom teeth knew and accepted the fact that being the youngest she could learn seventy-five per cent and teach twenty-five, Prudence proud at what I said and the way I said it because I was hers. And Mamma—it's hard to describe Mamma—you probably think of her as a pleasant middle-aged lady, complaisant and mildly permissive. No. For one thing, she has Prudence's face. It's older but not less. Just as beautiful, only it shows more living. Same curling hair, same build. The arms are a little looser, the waist a little thicker, but otherwise the same, just a body that's been around more. I mean, I don't want to sound horny or anything, but on a desert island I could go for Mamma as well as for Prudence, the only drawback being that Mamma wouldn't last as long. And I want Prudence to last long. I want her to outlast me, so I'll never be without her. Am I in love? Huh? I hope it doesn't impair my taste for obscenity. Fuck it, never! Anyway, we left early because Mr. Pudgybald had to catch a morning plane, drove back through the green-smelling night. The trees would break and show the moon and the shimmering river, and he'd sigh, and there were moments when I felt like kicking him out of the car. I mean, it should have been, could have been, Prudence beside me. But the Old Stoic in me saved him. I listened. He works for Standard Oil as a kind of welfare expert. Wherever Standard Oil goes he goes and makes suggestions about what American personnel need in the way of social and cultural activity, education for the children, how single men are likely to fare sexually, how friendly the local people are, whether they accept newcomers, what to do about it if they don't. It's a kind of undefined and important job. He splits his time between America and foreign stations, and the way he lives was a revelation. He's a kind of professional bachelor. He met Prudence's mother at a neighbor's, a dame who wanted to bring the lonely widow and civilized bachelor together. Little did she realize that Mr. Pudgybald was a pro, giving in to every housewife's compulsion to marry him off, to the extent of exchanging his wares, which are an experience of the world and a clever way of expressing himself, for good food, good liquor and a good audience. Maybe near the end, when he wants to stop working, he'll settle for the wealthiest widow or aged maiden about, but till then he'll travel along on other people's illusions and expectations. He didn't say any of this, mind you, but it was plain from the texture of his life as he unrolled the cloth and I rubbed my hand on it. So I learned something last night, that there are good lives possible outside the compass of Hollywood, priests, my mother, and myself for that matter. I don't know what Mr. Pudgybald's sex life is like, or even if he has any. But I doubt that it's important to him. He chooses to touch life lightly. And life, I expect, rather appreciates that for a change. Tonight about eight o'clock I was going out for some beer, and who should come up the front steps but Mary. What a wonderful surprise! Gee whiz, gosh almighty, holy mackerel, I said, desperately trying to think up quick answers for all the questions in her eyes. Which were, why hadn't I answered the letter she sent me, why hadn't I phoned, why hadn't I visited—in short, why hadn't I acted like the engaged man I am? I mean, if you ask a girl to marry you, and the girl says yes, it's reasonable to assume you're engaged, right? It reminded me of my relationship with the library when I was a kid. They'd send me cards, then letters, then they'd phone. Please return the book. The tone of their communications ran from formal to puzzled to outraged. But nothing worked. The book would be worth, say, three bucks, and as these pressures built up, I'd figure that soon they'd conclude they were throwing good energy after bad and forget me. They never did. They'd get to my parents, just as Mary, my mother told me, had been calling her every few days for news of me. With the library, it got so that when my mother woke me in the morning she'd remind me to return the book that day, and when my father came home from work at night the first thing he'd ask was whether I had returned the book. It began to seem that the whole world was focusing its attention on getting me to return the book—not that I wanted the goddamned thing at that point. Well, in the same way I had been hoping that if I didn't get in touch with Mary she would forget about me. Jesus, I didn't know what to say to her. Fortunately she provided a gambit. I think I know what you've been going through, she said. A religious crisis, haven't you? Yes, I said. I knew it, I knew I couldn't force you to confession and expect you to change overnight. I guess that's right, I said. I want to tell you something, something that may sound funny coming from me. What, I asked. I want to tell you that I'm sorry I made you go to confession. I went of my own accord, I said. No, no, I forced you, I had no right to, I had no right to say I'd marry you only if you were a Catholic. They're two different things, getting married and being a Catholic, she said. Well, I don't know if they are, I said, you have a perfect right to want to marry a Catholic, there might be all sorts of difficulties if you were a Catholic and I wasn't. Maybe there would be, she said, but that's still no excuse for me forcing you the way I did. Maybe not, I said. No maybes about it, and that's what I came here to tell you. So Mary was in my apartment, and she still had that great face. We were sitting on the couch, I leaned over and kissed her and she burst out crying. Well, I patted her on the back and kissed her and patted her on the back and before long I had her blouse off and then her bra and before longer I was lying beside her. I mean, the great face and the injured eyes and the honey hair on the dirty couch cover and the skinny shoulders and the frightened boobies—I'm not willing to say I love her or loved her but she got to me. And there was no resistance, nothing, I moved along at my own pace. I don't know if she enjoyed it or if she just thought it was OK for engaged couples, but I could do anything I wanted, so I put my hand on her rosebush finally. What are you doing, she said, and it wasn't a rhetorical question, she really wanted to know what I was doing. She was so appalled that I was appalled. I retreated, but after a while I pressed her skirted to me, and voom. Well, then about three hours ago, we were still lying there and Harvey knocked on the door. Mary rushed through the bedroom, trailing garments like pennants in the wind, and locked herself in the bathroom. But old eagle-eye knew immediately that I was, as they say, not alone. He spoke out in a loud formal voice about the weather and national news while making obscene gestures toward the bedroom. I told him he was mistaken, and to prove it opened the bedroom door. She had dropped a shoe, it lay like a roadsign in front of the bathroom. I tried dragging him out— he had flopped on the couch—but he hooked his legs over the arm. After a while, when I thought Mary would be crazy with anxiety in the bathroom, I went in to talk to her through the locked door. It's only Harvey, I said, and he knows we are engaged, there's nothing to be ashamed about. Get rid of him, she said, can't you get rid of him? He thinks it's another girl, I said, he's convinced it's another girl, and he wants to find out who. Did you tell him it was me? Yes, I said, but it's OK, we're engaged. Ooo, she said. I couldn't let him think I was fooling around with someone else, I said, and this seemed to touch her, so that in five minutes she emerged, reconstructed but white-faced, with great hauteur, which amused the hell out of Harvey, so that he treated her with elaborate politeness. I could have rapped him, because she accepted the politeness at face value, which amused him even more. Anyway, we drove her home, the three of us crowded over the bucket seats, and when she got out she gave me the kind of kiss that meant all was well with us. Then I drove Harvey home, and he told me the latest with his aging paramour, but I'm weary, man, it will have to wait.

＊ ＊ ＊ ＊ ＊ ＊ ＊ DID I WORK TODAY! I have my poor slob hero, whom, by the way, I decided to name Austin in honor of the Healey, out of the house. He's roaming the streets, snatching crumbs from frankfurter rolls on frankfurter stands, afraid that before they're digested someone will see them floating around on the surface of the contents of his stomach. The hot pavements burn, dirt adheres to sole and heel, so that he has to slide his feet along rather than pick them up, which would shock passers-by with the sight of moving footprints. I get Austin to his parents' home. Isn't that a great name, even apart from the Healey, it's a real slob's name. Anyway, his mother is out shopping. He gobbles up half a pound of sliced ham, drinks a quart of milk and watches the mess slowly dissolve as it becomes part of him. Even there, though, this poor baby has to hide in the closet after eating. Suppose his mother were to return suddenly and see a stomach full of milky masticated ham walking around. In the closet he begins to dream again. As soon as he pulls himself together he'll sneak aboard a transcontinental plane and fly to Moscow, where he'll hang around barbershops and street corners until he picks up the language. Then he'll enter the Kremlin, station himself in the bedroom of the head of state. Whispering in the dark of night, Austin will represent himself as a divine voice and thus begin to direct Russian foreign policy. He can see it now, Russia will make peaceful overtures to America. They'll be received with suspicion. So Austin will fly to Washington to do his stuff on the President. In fact he goes wherever there is trouble in the world, always in the cause of peace and justice. Within a year's time mankind has achieved a state of well-being unique in history. He reveals his accomplishments. Statues are raised to him in the world capitals. The Church canonizes him while he's still alive. And all the time he's dreaming like this he is trying to figure out answers to the simplest problems of life. Where can he live safely? How get food? How avoid capture by the scientists? Well, he decides to phone his buddy, whom I'm calling Schaefer in honor of the beer. Austin wants him to come over immediately. Schaefer wants Austin to come over to his place. Let's meet halfway at a bar, Schaefer suggests. Austin can't, Schaefer must come to him, and he shouldn't be surprised by what he sees or doesn't see, he adds mysteriously. This intrigues Schaefer, he tries to get Austin to explain. Austin won't, and Schaefer thinks he knows what it is: Austin's parents are away, he is shacking up with a nymphomaniac and needs his assistance to keep her content. Austin says nothing to disabuse him of the idea. Schaefer will be right over. While he waits, Austin again daydreams. With the help of a smart front man like Schaefer, he can become the richest and most powerful man in the world. That very night, they could, or Austin could, break into a store and steal money, with which Schaefer can buy things. Austin could hang around the safe of a large business firm and memorize the combination. The possibilities are limitless, and Schaefer would be appreciative enough and loyal enough to keep his mouth shut. What was it anyway that the two of them wanted from the world? In their many discussions about life they had decided that the only undeniable good was having women. So, after they got money, Schaefer would rent him a luxurious apartment and become his procurer. Schaefer could tell the girls that his client was a rich celebrity whose identity must remain a secret. The girls would have to consort with him in a perfectly dark room, for which service of course they would be handsomely paid. At such prices the girls were bound to be gorgeous creatures. It would be a shame not to get a look at them before the festivities. In fact if he didn't get a look at them he might as well hire cheap twenty-five or fifty-dollar girls. Ah, he had an idea. Suppose he answers the door himself, making out that it is being opened by remote control. He could even speak to the girls in a lighted room by explaining that he was using a high-fidelity intercom system. He would have a cocktail ready for them, and then after a bit of this intercom chatter he would direct them to undress, and finally they would be invited into the room of rooms, whose entrance is a maze-like light baffle to avoid the possibility of a door opening and giving him away in the saddle. There was, of course, the chance that the girls might come to the idea that he was a crook hiding out. This could lead to difficulties. Or curiosity might overcome one of them, and she would sneak a flashlight or match into the room. As he was enjoying these possibilities, the bell rang. He thought it was Schaefer and opened the door slowly so as not to frighten his friend. Instead, it was a young and beautiful girl. Apparently she thought the door had swung open by itself, and called into the apartment that she is collecting for Catholic Charities. When there was no answer from Austin and she seemed ready to go, he tiptoed into the kitchen, cupped his hands over his mouth to give the impression of greater distance and called for her to come in, he would be with her in a minute. Then he stepped out into the hall to see if she had followed his directions. She had, she even ran her hands over her butt to smooth her skirt and stuck out her breasts to tuck in her blouse. Austin was overwhelmed by her prettiness, by her cleanness and freshness. He could smell from eight or ten feet the feminine scents of powder and soap. The two of them stood silently facing one another for perhaps thirty seconds, until finally the girl became uneasy. Are you still there, she asked. Austin was too close to answer. I'll have to be going now, she called, and Austin was touched by a sense of great impending loss. At that moment he wanted this girl to stay with him more than he had wanted anything in his life. It wasn't only that she was pretty and open and innocent, it was particularly that she had come on a charitable mission. This meant she was a charitable person. He felt that if somehow without frightening her he could explain his situation she would stay and be his friend. But unless he did something in the next few seconds she would be gone and he would never see her again. He could not let that happen, so he slipped past her down the hall, slammed the door and threw the double lock. As soon as he saw the girl's face he was sorry. After an instant of shocked immobility, she rushed to the door, hands outstretched. Deep in her throat she made sounds of panic. Now he wanted her to get out, but in her haste and upset she kept unlocking one lock and locking the other. She couldn't seem to get them both open at the same time, and he didn't know how to help her. In his own agitation he knocked his elbow against the wall. At the noise the girl spun around, gave up the door and rushed into the living room. Afraid that she might jump from the window, Austin ran after and caught her by the waist. His touch brought on a hysterical seizure. She shook convulsively, and her sounds died to desperate breathing. Austin hurried back to the door, unlocked it and threw it open. She passed him and was gone like a bird from a cage. He was all shame and remorse. He had to go after her to discover the extent of the damage he had done. There she was, in front of the building, near collapse in the arms of a middle-aged woman who was patting her and crooning There, there. From the girl came a mixture of gasps and wails. A crowd gathered, a policeman arrived. Eventually the girl quieted down and told her story. As soon as the cop elicited the number of the apartment he trotted into the building. In a few minutes he was back leading Schaefer by the arm. Schaefer's face showed both guilt and fright, but also anger. Apparently he thought Austin had played some terrible joke on him. So what do you think, man? See, I want to cut off Austin's various accesses to salvation. I'm going to isolate him more and more, really put the screws to him, push him right to the edge. What will happen then I don't know, something, we'll see. So much for art. Friday night Harvey showed up to talk about his forthcoming marriage. Forthcoming meaning yesterday afternoon in the chambers of one Judge Arnold Barfman. Harvey's ladylove actually got the divorce, by the way. I didn't know what to say to Harvey. I mean, he's twenty-one, as who isn't, and if he wants to marry this aged objet d'amour, well, all right. And I would, as requested, be best man. I showed him the suit I planned to wear, a nice dark gray tropical worsted, as well as the white shirt and the blue tie with discreet diagonal stripes and the black shoes and the ribbed nylon socks, and asked him what he was wearing. He just shook his head and grunted. Are you going through with this thing or not, I said, because if you're not, tell me, so I can line something up for tomorrow. I needed a strong weekend for myself, I felt a rather large loneliness gathering with the dust-balls under the bed, and I wanted to keep moving. Well, he'd just nod and grunt, the most neutral nod and grunt I ever saw. This was not the happy anticipation one expects from a bridegroom. Not that I blamed him. In the first place his parents knew nothing about the marriage, he told them he was moving in with his musical-comedy collaborator. Also, the bride's lawyers had never approached him with a settlement. Also, Foxy had not come through with the ten-grand honorarium. Not that I blamed Fox either. I mean, this was a business deal, and Madam Fox had already gotten the divorce. Fox could marry his chick without offending Mrs. Fox's moneybag brother. So it looked like a sick crummy world to me, and Harvey did not look like he was making his way in it. I mean, Harvey can do some outrageous things, but they always seemed to be things to talk about, like going into Christian Science Reading Rooms and asking for the lavatory. Harvey was the cueball, sending other balls on their way, but here he was rolling into the pocket himself. Do you love her, I asked. She's a crazy good screw, he said. But do you love her? I love a crazy good screw, he said. That's not going to help you at the dinner table, I said, and he wouldn't answer me, just grunt and nod. Well, this was a poor baby if I ever saw one, so I decided to interfere, be a kind of anti-Cupid. I fed him liquor. By two in the morning he'd had three-fourths of a quart, and I had had the rest. I could hardly keep my eyes open, but Harvey kept going and going. We went for a ride in the Austin-Healey, which, by the way, we got up to a hundred. I didn't, he did, and I only knew it because he told me later. But I do remember that just before we got back he said he had to pee. We pulled over, he took an almost empty pint of Canadian Club from the glove compartment, drank the contents, and peed into the neck. Peed into the neck somewhat, that is. Most went on the floor. He put the cap back on and tucked the bottle under the car. Well, I was sure he'd pass out when I got him home and maybe he'd sleep through the wedding. But he no sooner flopped on the couch than he sprang up and announced that we had to go out again. Some bum might find the bottle and think it was whiskey, he said. Well, we never found the bottle, and maybe some bum did think it was whiskey, but Harvey has a good heart, I say. I mean, if it had even occurred to me about the bum, I'd have said the hell with it, do him good, but Harvey is conscientious. So finally we got back the second time, after picking up beer on the way, and instead of falling down in a bunch, he got out my phonograph records. I was the one who passed out, and I would have slept through the wedding, if at one-thirty yesterday afternoon he hadn't woke me up.

He was all shaved and dressed, and he shoved me into the shower, and I put on my gray suit and my black shoes and my white shirt and my blue tie and we went to the chambers of Judge Arnold Barfman. Not to keep you in suspense, let me say that Harvey isn't married. Apparently after I got to sleep he went out and bought still more beer, and by the time we made the courthouse the poor slob was totally white and totally silent. He didn't wobble or anything, and he'd give me a little dig if I put my hand on his elbow to steady him, but all the zing was gone. The bride was there, in a tailored suit, pulled in at the waist. I had never seen her before, and she looked pretty good, but not to marry, for Chrissake. I mean, she had a big ass and big tits and alligator shoes and a leathery tan face and hair dyed the color of expensive wood and a gay corsage and a brother and two friends—a man and woman somewhere between her age and Harvey's—and I'm sure she's a crazy good screw, but she could have been Harvey's mother. In fact she and Foxy have a nineteen-year-old daughter. Where was the daughter, I thought, bring on the daughter, at least Harvey would have a chance with the daughter. But this was a monster, and everybody knew it. The brother was an oily runt who looked disgusted with the whole thing, and the couple, who I guess were supposed to be witnesses, were smily and nervous and gave the impression of being thrilled to be so near big money. The judge was an impassive fart with a hairline mustache, hired to officiate, aware that he was expected to add fatherly authority to the proceedings. Well, my outrage was unnecessary, because some of the scene must have gotten through to Harvey. We weren't in the room a minute when he slumped into the chair and wouldn't, or couldn't, get up. He didn't pass out, mind you, but he didn't acknowledge the introductions or the pleasantries of the witnessing couple either, or the frowns of the brother. I guess the brother and I felt the same way about the thing. Harvey gave the bride a few deadpan glances, but otherwise he just stared at the knees of whoever stood in front of him. After a while, they got a doctor, a house physician from a nearby hotel, who said that Harvey was in alcoholic shock. The doctor gave him a shot of vitamin B or something, and the male witness helped me get him down to the car. Harvey didn't say a mumbling word all the way home, and he listed like a broken boat going up the stairs. But in the apartment he finally passed out. I went over to the tennis court near the river, worked up a sweat and sort of shook off the night. Harvey came to about eleven P.M. and asked for a drink, and when I said there was nothing around he passed out again. This morning he was gone. I felt like a Boy Scout, I had done my good undeed.

⁕ ⁕ ⁕ ⁕ ⁕ ⁕ ⁕ MONDAY NO HARVEY at MUI, and I didn't know how to get in touch with him. If I called his home and he wasn't there, I might worry his parents. Tuesday no Harvey. Wednesday no Harvey. The art director hadn't heard from him, picture proofs were piling up on his desk. Wednesday afternoon Fox called me to his office and said he was surprised I was still working for him and not writing for television. I don't think I'd be any good at that, sir, I said. You don't think you'd be any good at it? No, sir. You mean you think you'd be too good, don't you? I didn't answer him, I was wondering what I had done to call this forth. May I speak to you frankly, he said. Sure. If you were a Jewish boy—you're not a Jewish boy, are you—if you were a Jewish boy we'd say you had a goyische kopf, do you know what that means? Yes, I said. I don't mean the words, I mean the idea, do you know what the idea means? Yes. Well, and he sighed, if you know what the idea means, you don't have one. That doesn't necessarily follow, I said. Believe me, it follows, will you believe me if I say it follows, if I say it follows will you believe me? OK, if you say so, I said. You see, if you had a goyische kopf, you'd argue with me, wouldn't you? Whatever you say, I said. OK, now the caption writer is not coming back. How come? He's an unstable boy, if you want the job it's yours. Thank you. Wait, before you accept I'd like to ask you a question, may I ask you a question? Sure. Why are you here? Here, I asked. Here at MUI, because if you're here to make money the only thing you'll make is a mistake. I asked him why that was so. If you wrote me fifty articles a day, a hundred captions, collected a thousand pictures, if you did any one of those jobs outside—and he waved his hand in deprecation of his staff—like a genius, you wouldn't make money. I asked him again why this was so. Because I wouldn't pay you money. If you were a genius, a genius, I'd only pay you two, three hundred a week. Isn't that a lot of money, I asked. If you're a genius, it's a lot of money. I'm not a genius, I said. You're lucky, can I tell you something? Sure. To make money, there's one thing you have to do, do you know what that is? Marry it, I said. You're a deep boy. So there are two ways, what's the other way? Steal it. I'm a busy man, I'm taking time to tell you something, do you want to learn or joke? Learn, I said. All right, you sell, and he paused for my reaction. My father was a salesman, I said. He made money? Yes. Of course, he said. Do all salesmen make money, I said. Some salesmen don't sell, my friend. Your father was a selling salesman, so he made money. I can look at you and know your father made money, do you know how I know? How? Because you're a nicely brought-up boy. Your father made money and sent you to a nice school, didn't he? Pretty nice, I said. But he didn't want you to be a salesman like him. I don't know about that, I said, when he retired he asked me if I wanted his job, because if I did he said he'd hold out until I was finished school and he could turn over his territory to me. And you said what? I said I wanted to be a writer. And he said what when you said you wanted to be a writer. He said I'd have to pick something I could make a living at. And you said? I said I'd be a teacher. But you didn't want to be a teacher. No. You wanted to be a writer. Yes. And what do you want now? To be a writer. So what are you doing in the art department? Making a living. A good living? It's OK. But you'd rather be a writer. Yes. Do you want to write captions? Sure. Your heart's desire is to write captions. It's not my heart's desire particularly. You're too good to write captions. I didn't say that. But you thought it. Does anybody want to write captions, Mr. Fox? No, so why not admit it? All right, I don't want to write captions. You just turned down a good job, he said. Mr. Fox, you've been frank with me, may I be frank with you? His eyes narrowed, he thought I was going to insult him, but Go ahead, he said. I heard you address the staff when I worked here the first time, and you said that books were the hardest commodity in the world to sell. So? So if that's true, couldn't you make more money selling stocks or groceries or something else besides books? Did I say I was interested in making money, he said. No. So what's your point? I guess I don't have any point, but may I say something else, Mr. Fox? Go. Well, I think you have a goyische kopf, which made him laugh, and after that I kind of liked the guy. Anyway, it turned out that he didn't want me to write captions. He had been testing me. Actually he wanted me to work with him and another guy developing a sales program for MUI. Also, he told me that he was selling another item besides books, an item in which there was no profit at all, only satisfaction. It's the most valuable item in the world, see if you can guess what it is, he said. God, love, sex, I didn't know. I'm selling, he said, capitalism to Communists! His idea was to attack communism in the same way Communists were attacking capitalism, through salesmanship. Train agents in the dialectics of free enterprise and sneak them behind the Iron Curtain. Have them work their way into the state-owned factories, the collective farms, into the schools and newspapers, even into the government itself, just as Communists infiltrate into our institutions. (Shades of Austin.) Communists are the greatest salesmen the world has ever seen, he said, and we haven't learned from them. Well, the guy has two staff members on the scheme full time, working out the bugs, as he put it. And when the presentation is done he intends to send it to the President. If the President doesn't act on it, he'll send it to Congress. And if they do nothing, he'll take it directly to the people. He would prefer the secrecy of an Executive crash program but, whichever way, he feels it's bound to work. While I was in his office his former brother-in-law called, Fox's voice rose to a wheedling whine, the poor slob, and I gathered from the conversation that as publisher of MUI he felt he was not adequately endowed with university degrees. He had learned that a certain institution in Maryland would issue him an honorary Litt.D. in exchange for a donation of five thousand dollars' worth of books to their library, but he needed the brother-in-law's OK to charge it off to MUI. He didn't do much of a selling job that I could see, because after he hung up he said How will it look, that three people on my staff have Ph.D.'s when I only have a B.S.? Since I already told him that he had a goyische kopf I decided not to push my luck, and suggested that he pay for the books himself if he couldn't charge them to the company. He said he might have to, and added that at trade discount they'd only come to three thousand bucks. Well, he offered me this other job, and I accepted, which entitles me to a title, Assistant Director of Sales Research for the Revised Modern Universal International Encyclopedia, at $145 a week. Someone's at the door. It's Jose. More later, man. He just left, after telling me the secret of his life. He's in love with a nun who teaches in the grammar school across the street. In fact, that's why he's living here, to be close to her. Wait a minute, I want to go to the window and find out the name, also get a beer. I can't see the name, but it's something like School of the Sacred Heart or the Bloody Liver. I could see, however, carved over the two entrances, the word BOYS and the word GIRLS. Like great toilets. Did you know that the Catholic grammar schools separate the sexes after the fifth grade, shake the kiddies down into convex and concave, short-haired and long-haired, flat-assed and round-assed. Otherwise some devil-ensnared eleven-year-old Catholic male might just slip his foot, hand, pookie into a Catholic female's coozie. Let's consider the facts, man. There is no God. Or if there is one it's unlikely He resembles the God put forth by the Christian churches. I mean, because human beings have been projecting images of God like crazy for thousands of years the chances that this is the right one are not overwhelming. So what is a young girl doing when she becomes a nun, when she takes the vows of poverty, obedience and chastity? Most people are poor anyhow, and also obedient— to bosses, spouses, mores. But the chastity, ah, where else but in a religious community is celibacy institutionalized. Consider, this young girl is now provided with a complete change of rules. Where before she was at the doubtful mercy of those billions of penetrating males who roam the earth, offering her violence and violation, now they accept that she is off limits. And as a teacher she inculcates her former fears for herself into the children, she keeps the girls from the boys and the boys from themselves. Well, given this none condition, we find Jose in love with one. It makes me wonder. Seems the nun in question is his cousin. When he came to America five years ago he went to live with his father's brother's family. They had one child, Rita, eighteen, two years older than Jose. Now she is Sister Barbara, Jose says with disgust, they have taken the blood even from her name. The instant I saw her, he said, I fell in love. Limbs like burnished wood (we went to the beach often), a voice like the viola d'amore (she hummed as she washed the dishes after supper), exactly semispheric breasts (I surprised her in the bath on two occasions). Did she know you loved her, I asked. Of course she knew, when I looked at her she could feel me between her thighs. Does she know you're living across the street from her? Of course, every night I enter her cell and lie with her, every night she experiences my presence, and every morning she is on fire for the reality. I mean, does she consciously know you're here? I speak to her every day, every morning when she gathers the dirty-faced children on the sidewalk in double file I am there. In person? Of course, in person. Don't the other nuns get suspicious? They are suspicious of everyone, Jose said, malevolent penguins, suspicious and jealous. She tells them, however, that I am the father of one of her students. You don't look old enough, I said. That is why I have grown this mustache, but what does it matter, what can they do? One morning she will tear off the black cerements and come back with me to my room. What do you say when you talk to her? I tell about the night before, how firm and deep I was, how responsive and satisfying she was. Occasionally when I have had a woman in my room she will have sensed it and say nothing to me. Doesn't anyone overhear you? We speak Spanish, although there is one Puerto Rican boy, I will see him on the street alone one day and frighten him. What does she say to you? She pleads with me to leave her in peace, but this is the traditional reply of the woman, is it not? Always they say no, while pressing their flesh on your flesh. No, no, and then O, O. She is waiting for me now, I must go to my room. Good luck, I said. I do not need luck, he said, I need endurance. I think he needs both.

⁂ ⁂ ⁂ ⁂ ⁂ ⁂ ⁂ ⁂ ⁂ THIS WEEK WE began testing MUI's Experimental Plan for the Development of Direct Sales Technique. The site is a block of lower-middle-class five-story apartment houses that in ten years will be slummy furnished rooms. Now, however, they contain the ideal customers for educational products: uneducated parents eager for the advancement of their children, parents who don't have the background to judge the quality of what you're selling, parents who feel vague guilt about not having provided a richer cultural home environment, parents who because of their general ignorance revere books, and finally deprived parents who hunger for all goods. This isn't my explanation, it's an abstract of the theorizing of my immediate superior at MUI, the Director of the Plan, a little mutt named Wally. Wally is about five feet four with a gray flabby face and a withered arm. Of the commodities he's sold I can remember jewelry, candy, socks, life insurance, pencils, vacuum cleaners, virgin forests, mutual securities, cemetery plots, round-the-world tours, cigars and mailing lists. Fox claims that Wally is one of the ablest salesmen he has ever met, a pure salesman, that is, a salesman who can sell anything. The quaintest attribute of this one-and-a-half-armed bandit, considering the line he's in now, is that he don't talk English good. Like, that may be your point of contention, I've got other convictions on the matter which it may be to our mutual benefit to inquire. I've listened to him for hours, and I imagine he really is good. In the first place, he's so ugly he's beautiful, like an English pug or a frog. I have a feeling he could go into the crummiest tenement in the city and the people would be joyous they weren't him. When he speaks it's like listening to a member of another species, consequently you treasure his words and gestures. He was showing me how, at the right point, you slip a pen to the customer so he can sign the contract half-consciously. He gave me the pen with his withered hand. That's the ace he keeps up his sleeve. The only time he referred to himself in a genuinely personal way he said You know why I like this game? I like pulling the wool over these so-called wise guys' eyes. A sweetheart, huh? Well, let us see how I gather information for the Development of Direct Sales Technique. At ten A.M. (which gives the superintendent an opportunity to get the garbage out, pick up the used rubber behind the stairwell, remove pee and bubble gum from the elevator floor, and have his breakfast) I descend into the bowels of my building. Before ringing I carefully note the superintendent's name, since I will be addressing him as Mister So-and-So throughout the interview. I will explain that I am a member of the Junior Research Educators' Association. Would he be kind enough to provide me with the names of families having children of grammar and high school age? I am making an important study of educational usage in the neighborhood, and his cooperation will be of greatest value. If he should require identification—one cannot be too careful nowadays—I have a letter on embossed stationery stating that I am myself and that the results of my inquiry will be used in a nationwide study to the purpose of raising the intellectual standards of tomorrow's citizens so that the country may be better equipped to meet the increasing threat of Russian technological advancement. The letter is signed by both the mayor and the governor. You figure out how Fox got the signatures, I can't. Clipped to the letter is a round-edged card bearing my picture and name, with all of which I feel I could interview the President's wife. But let us see what happens under actual battle conditions. The superintendent of the first building was named Rooney. I burned it into my brain and rang. A fat woman in housecoat answered. May I see your husband, madam, I am a member . . . My husband's dead. I'm very sorry to hear that, ma'am, may I see the superintendent then? You're looking at him. Mrs. Rooney? What you selling? I ignored this, announced my name and launched into a description of my mission. You selling books? No, I'm not selling books, Mrs. Rooney, and I began again to describe my mission. You want to know what kids in the building? Well, yes, Mrs. Rooney, but not to sell books, you see, I am engaged in collecting data for the Junior Research Educators' Association, and I withdrew my letter, which she took but did not read. Rose Goldhammer 3D, Peter See 1B, Louise Schneider 4B, Bobby, Shirley Kaltz 3A, and so on. Ten in all. And would you know by chance which schools these youngsters attend, and perhaps the grades they are in. Well, I had to slow her up to get it all down. Then I thanked her profusely, adding that her help and the help of people like her would eventually do a great deal toward meeting the challenge of international communism. That's a little of their own back, she said. What do you mean, Mrs. Rooney? I mean getting me up in the middle of the night to fix a toilet. Fifty-six dollars' rent entitles them to me closing stuck windows, cleaning pilot lights, changing fuses, listening about a crack in the wall six months till the bastard owns this place pays five bucks to the plasterer. Do me a favor, will you, sonny? I certainly will, Mrs. Rooney, anything you say. Sell the kikes, they're the worst, and she slammed the door. Nobody answered at 1B. O, by the way, I have a brief case that weighs a hundred and eighty-five pounds, so maybe Wally's short arm isn't a short arm at all, maybe his other arm is a long arm from carrying such brief cases. Therein is a big leather looseleaf folder containing about forty pages and six mammoth foldouts, Volume One of MUI, which is the only one yet printed, and a miniature tape recorder. At 3D I reached into the brief case and turned it on. Then I straightened my tie and rang. Who is it? And here I had my first proof of Wally's genius. If they want to know who it is, he said, sing out your name. I did, the door flew open. Mrs. Goldhammer, I said to the skinny, sort of pretty woman. Yes? Does Rose Goldhammer live here? Yes, apprehensively. Is she the Rose Goldhammer in the seventh grade at Herman Melville Junior

High? Yes, now biting her lip. Nothing to worry about, Mrs. Goldhammer, I'm from the Junior Research Educators' Association and I'd like to see you and Mr. Goldhammer and Rose together tonight. Will eight o'clock be all right? Yes, her face all questions. See you then, eight o'clock, and swiftly I scooped up my brief case, down the stairs. You can't wait for an elevator, questions are lethal, you must get away from the scene of the crime immediately. With the same method I fixed up nine o'clock with Mrs. Schneider, mother of Louise. Done for the day. But not for the night. At eight I was back. The Goldhammer menage was spotless and in a way that made me think it wasn't spotless often. Mrs. Goldhammer was attired in what might be called a cocktail dress. Mr. Goldhammer, heavy-jawed and newly shaven, had on tie, jacket and frown. Rose was in her holiday best, looking as if whatever she had been doing or not doing at school was about to catch up with her. Mr. Goldhammer had a German-Jewish or Middle-European accent. He bowed as he shook my hand, and indicated the most comfortable chair. No, Mr. Goldhammer, I'd like us all to sit on the couch if you don't mind, perhaps you could be on my right. Rose, here on my left. And, Mrs. Goldhammer, would you be beside Rose. There now, and I took out the looseleaf folder, all of whose ideas had been lifted from the sales-promotion material of four other encyclopedias. Page One described in letters that could be read six feet away the general purpose of the Junior Research Educators' Association. This I read aloud slowly, interrupting myself every now and then with a question, such as You agree that the most important natural resource of the free world is its children, do you not, Mr. Goldhammer? Yess, yess, and he slapped his thigh for emphasis. Page Two contained three words writ even larger KNOWLEDGE IS FREEDOM. Thereafter every other page or so was dedicated to such a sentiment, whose purpose is diabolically various. If the customer seems to enjoy being lectured, you elucidate. But if he's nodding you along in a yeah-yeah fashion, you merely say something like No truer words were ever spoken, and turn the page. If you feel he needs to assert himself, you ask his opinion of the sentiment, and then after a little tacit resistance you say I think you're right, you know, I think you're right. Then there is an occasional page devoted to the biography of a self-educated man like Lincoln, with appropriate quotations about what books and learning meant to him. The first foldout was a great map of the United States showing the extent of the activities of the Association. O and there was a list of quiz-program-type questions, which you address to the child. A sure winner. If the kid does well, you praise the parents for the obvious care they are taking with their offspring. If the kid's a dope, you gently indicate that unless something is done the child may not realize his full potential in adult life. Rose was either a dope or nervous, and Mr. Goldhammer began rubbing his hands together as if he planned to use them on her when I left. Luckily my next page said YOUTH IS CURIOSITY, and I explained that a twelve-year-old's mind is an eager vacuum, a hungry animal, an unused muscle, which settled Mr. Goldhammer down some. Things were flipping along until I came to Foldout Three, a life-size four-color picture of all of MUI's thirty-six projected volumes. I put the folder on the floor and spread the handsome illustration on the rug. As I leaned over to point at various features, Mr. Goldhammer's foot came down on volumes twenty-two, twenty-three, and twenty-four. I looked up. His teeth were bared. You're a gottamned book salesman, and he pulled the knot of his tie away from his neck. Fake gottamned book salesman. He got to his feet, both of which were now on the foldout. You're a gottamned junior-association book salesman selling books here and get out before I call the policeman. Rose had retreated to one corner, Mrs. Goldhammer to another. I got to my feet, also on the foldout. I resent what you're implying very much, Mr. Goldhammer. I have never sold a book in my life. I take a solemn oath on that, and if that is how you repay the time, money and interest the Junior Research Educators' Association is spending on your daughter's development—I leave my own time and energy out—well, all I can say is I wish you well. Yes, I wish you and Rose well, and I hope that when the occasion arises, as it will, that America and the rest of the free world must match its cultural and scientific achievements against those of our mortal enemies, the task does not fall to you, Mr. Goldhammer. That's all I can say. But it wasn't enough, because although he had been silenced for a moment it was plain he was gathering his English for another assault. Ah, but here Wally's genius proved itself again.

I pulled from my brief case Volume One of MUI and turned to the last page of the front matter, where under Editorial Consultants stood my name heading the list. Out came my letter and identification card. Do these look like the credentials of what you so brashly and perhaps libelously called a goddamned book salesman? He took the book and papers. The letter didn't mean a thing, or the card, it was my name in the book. How many people have their names in a book for millions to see, for history to remember? Genius, I tell you. This was the Experimental part of the Plan. When MUI is finally finished, every (you should pardon the expression) salesman will have a Volume One with his name listed as editorial consultant. The fact that there might be a thousand salesmen around the country pushing MUI is no difficulty. Space would be left open and specially printed like a calling card, and the set that was eventually sent to the customer would also have the salesman's name. Well, I tell you, before the evening was over—it went on to midnight, so that I had to call up Mrs. Schneider and cancel out for nine—I had drunk Mr. Goldhammer's whiskey, and advised Rose on high schools and college, watched Mrs. Goldhammer model her new coat for me, and accepted an invitation for dinner two weeks hence. I was also given the name of four of Mr. Goldhammer's friends with school-age children, and he promised to call them beforehand to avoid similar misunderstandings. Of course, I don't know how it would have gone if I really tried to sell him some books. As it was, I only had to bring back a recording of the interview. The tape had run out at ten o'clock, but the two hours I had, Wally, Fox and I listened to the next day in Fox's office. They decided to remove the offending foldout, and they said that I too was a genius. Should I be proud or ashamed?

⚹ ⚹ ⚹ ⚹ ⚹ ⚹ ⚹ ⚹ LAST NIGHT WAS Catholic night. My Catholic but otherwise human mother has been after me to see a childhood friend named Francis, who is studying to be a priest. I say childhood friend, but he was just a fringe member of the gang, always a bit separate, a bit precious. My most vivid recollection of Francis is a time some kid broke his glasses and a piece of glass got stuck in his eye. For six months afterward his mother came out after school with him, and that was his undoing, I think. No one broke his glasses again, but then no one wanted to either. Looking back on it, it was then that he turned to adults, turned his talents to pleasing and getting along with them. In the last year of high school he disappeared, and when the following summer we heard that he was going into the seminary, we understood why he had kept to himself. He could hardly have hung around with us on street corners cunt-baiting, planning seductions that never came off, working up the nerve to visit a cat house. It's funny, I had left the Church three years before, when I was fourteen, but even then, at seventeen, I was awed at Francis's decision to become a priest. All of us, as cynical and tumid as we were, were deeply impressed. It was really something to give up the potential of the adult world for the priesthood. Potential? At seventeen, that meant quiff. My mother has never pressed me about having left the Church, which I guess was part of her arrangement with my father, no overt religionizing. But I'm sure she harbors fond wishes for my return to the fold, and I suspect that my meeting with Francis, which she arranged, was part of a secret scheme to get me back in touch with things sanctified. Well, I picked him up at her place and took him to the nicest restaurant in the neighborhood, the kind of restaurant the local judge takes his wife to once a week and ordinary wage earners celebrate their wedding anniversaries at, and we were given the finest treatment because of Francis's as yet un- earned Roman collar. The captain knew him and his parents and made a great thing over him and me, placed us at a quiet roomy table, came over with every course to see how it was going. Our waiter was a big Italian- American in his late twenties, a smoothy, a tough, a cocksman, whose true values obviously didn't coincide with the Church's. I don't know, but I'll tell you what kind of guy he struck me as, married probably, three kids—which was why he was waiting on table and not hanging around a candy store—but also he was banging some broad on the side, with ambitions to make it in the local annex of the Mafia. Get the picture? And yet he was overwhelmed at serving a man of the cloth. I felt like saying, paisan, spill the soup in this eunuch's lap, it's one thing for your wife and mother to defer to priests, but you're a big boy, you know better, grab your fly and ask him if he wants a bite, don't fawn on this nothing. Well, Francis took all the attention as if it was coming to him, and I made a discovery last night. I never understood the attraction of the priesthood before, but seeing this four-eyed, peckerless little vacuity opposite me, I realized what a magnificent solution it was for him. What would Francis be without that collar, without the skirts of the Church, the ready blessings, the power to loose and to bind, the mumbled Latin and the talismanic breviary? Either a fag, practicing or frustrated, or an impotent married man. In both cases his true situation would be apparent, and he would be the object of contempt for our big wop waiter. Even the mothers, the aging ladies of the parish, would know that something was amiss and avoid him, whisper about him, discreetly warn their sons away. I mean, maybe he'd run the local library, teach school or start a Boy Scout troop. But the mark would be on him. And if he married, he'd take to drink, finally shoot himself at forty. But now, here, Roman-collared, he was a master of the community. All loved him, all respected him. And if he has any humanness in him, as I suspect Francis has, he will be clever enough to make cutely sacrilegious jokes about the Pope, so that after he leaves the households of parishioners, where he has been served roast beef and rich red wine and homemade apple pie, all will say together Isn't

Father Francis a regular guy! The roughs, the big-nosed Irish souses, shame of their children, will say of him He's all right! Now, I'm not sure Francis has this talent, maybe he'll be a prissy priest, insisting on absurd proprieties, striving for unattainable virtues, but I don't think so. He swallows the social sweets too well. When we came into the restaurant, the captain said to him How's it coming along, then paused, wanting to use the proper term of address, but, not knowing what it was, simply smiled at the end of the question. And what did Francis say? St. Francis has not despaired of his namesake yet. O my hairy balls! St. Francis has not despaired of his namesake yet. Well, this priestling played me the same way, revealing little peccadilloes of his housemaster and his theology professor, how some fellow seminarians smoke on the sly, hints of jealousies and backbiting—all very human, you understand—but nothing at all about pulling their pricks into black socks in the quiet of the night, nothing about lusting after the new blond underclassman's rectal aperture. Jesu, I don't know why I should be furzerzled over so patent a nothing as potential Father Francis, except that someday he'll set up in a parish and titillate the nuns with his toothy smile and tell thirteen-year-old boys in the confessional that they are wasting their life's blood by laying hand on tool. I suppose there's just no being an ex-Catholic, you have to be an anti-Catholic. I wish sometimes I could be big about religion, see the greater wisdom in it for the masses, see it as an unconscious folk creation that gives the common man the only dignity he's likely to get on earth. But I can't, I've been a victim, and when I think of Mary with her fanaticism, which in forty years will be an ancient crankiness, I could cry. Well, after dinner, during which Francis much patted lips with napkin and belly with hand, already adopting the manner of the mouth-centered middle-aged monsignor, I took him downtown to my digs. What else to do with him? He was on leave from the seminary because his mother had died, and he wanted something more from the evening, some other benefit. And through the purest good fortune, who should come to my door but Jose. I drafted him, excellent fellow. Seeing that I had company, at first he wanted to flee, but seeing more closely that my company was collared by Rome, he drafted gladly. What an evening! He fetched the remainder of the cognac I had given him, as well as his latest Very Tale, and proceeded to do his stuff. As the wind of time, he said, continues to blow against man, loosening his grip at the top of the evolutionary ladder, only the Church can maintain him. God in His infinite wisdom has created this institution to save us from history. Do you realize, Father—I had explained that Francis was only a seminarian, but Jose chose not to hear—that only the Church allows men to be human, allows them to err. All other orthodoxies demand perfection. If I am an intellectual, my taste must be faultless. If I am a Communist, my views must never vary from the State's. If I am a liberal, I must be tolerant even of reaction. Only Mother Church allows for imperfection, and thus she will be mankind's salvation. Mother Church understands that man is weak, that he lusts and envies, hates and covets, doubts and despairs, that he has an animal heritage. I admire fascism, do my progressive friends permit me this? I believe the world is in a stranglehold of Jewish conspiracy, do my Jewish friends forgive me this? I have a certain distaste for the flesh of woman, which you yourself no doubt understand, Father, will my psychoanalytically oriented friends let me lie? They insist that I lay. And then, in honor of Father Francis, Jose read his latest Very Tale, a wild story about a Spanish priest, which he claims will show children the strange ways of God's will. It seems that after serving a small village in central Spain for some years this priest experienced a moral crisis. He came to the ugly conclusion that he was not accomplishing his mission. The peasants and petty merchants of his parish kept coming back to him, over and over again, with the same sins. This man was a thief, that woman an adulteress, their sins seemed to be part of their characters. O they were always repentant at the time of confession, always determined to do better in the future, but what good was this when he knew their intentions would come to nothing? It got so that he could tell almost to the day when a given parishioner would turn up with his or her particular sin. He berated them for their frailty, imposed severe penances, described the terrors of damnation, and they would weep and beg forgiveness and make resolutions. But always, in a week, a month, a year, they came back. He even tried withholding absolution from the worst offenders, but one of them died. The priest was overwhelmed with remorse, feeling that he personally was accountable for the man's damnation, and he made a special trip to Madrid to see his bishop. Well, the bishop was a worldly type and told the priest not to worry about the dead man, that his desire to confess was no doubt sufficient to have gained him preferment in the afterlife. For the future, however, the bishop warned, the priest must not withhold absolution except in the most extraordinary circumstances. These are simple people, the bishop explained, they cannot see too far ahead, and, besides, he should have more faith in God's mercy and the machinery of the Church. Well, this didn't satisfy the priest. He returned to his village and consulted Canon Law, which plainly states that a man dying in mortal sin is damned, and he knew only too well that most of his flock were hardly cool from confession before they returned to their evil ways. Now it so happened that shortly after his trip to Madrid one of the greatest sinners in the village came to the priest to confess. This man confessed once a year like clockwork, just before Easter, and each time he was loaded with enough transgressions to damn him ten times over. To make matters worse the man was in bad health. He would surely die before another year had passed. There was only one thing to do. After hearing the man's sins and giving him absolution, the priest followed him home and on a lonely stretch of road dispatched him with a piece of broken pew he had taken along for the purpose. Now, on the one hand, the priest was cast down because he had committed the first mortal sin of his life by killing another human being. On the other hand, he was joyous at having sent an otherwise lost soul to God. And even if he himself were to die at this moment, he reasoned, the score would be one up, one down—not bad if you consider that many are called and few are chosen. The next day he similarly saved an old lady. Now the score was two to one. Well, the priest was so stimulated by his success that he volunteered for missionary work in Africa, and there he did wonders. Assigned to a tiny tribe in the interior, he not only converted the natives to Christianity as Europeans practice it, he also sold them on his sure-fire salvation technique. As new babies were born he baptized them and clunked them on the head with the piece of pew. And the adults he didn't have to sneak up behind any more. They came to him voluntarily to be clunked off to heaven. Well, in a matter of two years he had the whole tribe safely established in paradise, and now that his work was done he decided it was his duty to return to civilization and seek forgiveness for himself. But it so happened that before he could reach another priest he succumbed to jungle fever and went to hell. There Satan, peeved at his achievements, committed him to a special part of hell where the torments were worse than in any other. Despite this dire punishment, however, the priest was completely happy, so great was his satisfaction at having saved two hundred and sixty-one souls for God. Well, I don't know whether it was the cognac or not, but Francis said that he thought in many ways it was a very beautiful story. Jose was delighted, and since I was falling asleep, he invited Francis back to his room, where, he said, he would read him his interpretation of Genesis, which showed that Eden was lost to man because Eve, overreaching herself, tried to seduce the Lord.

✖ ✖ ✖ ✖ ✖ ✖ ✖ ✖ ✖ ✖ LIFE IS FULL of surprises. Prudence is pregnant, which sounds like a contradiction in terms. She told me this little fact of nature at lunch today. She wouldn't tell me the details, however. When did you find out, I asked. Last week. Who's the guy? No answer. How long have you been pregnant? Nothing. Did it happen after you knew me or before? Are you going to marry the guy? Do you love him? Did she intend to have the baby? Would she bring it up herself. Was she still sleeping with the guy? How many times had she slept with him? Had she ever slept with anyone else? I just couldn't stop, and I asked her the questions as if I had a right to the answers. I mean, there was never any understanding between us. What went on went on in my head, and maybe in hers, but it stayed inside the heads. I didn't have any right to the answers, but I asked her and waited, and when no answer came I'd ask her another. I think I was trying to break her down so I could get close to her again because, Jesus, I suddenly felt like a complete stranger. But she didn't break, she just sat there and looked at me, pink cheeks white. Why did you tell me, if you won't tell me the whole thing? I thought you'd want to know, she said. I do, but I want to know the rest of it too, and I gave the table a little bang. I waited, she waited. Tell me, I said, and I smashed the table with my fist. Well, she jumped up and left, almost as if I had knocked her off the table like a vase. I know what you'll say, you'll say in your almost infinite wisdom that it wasn't her and the other guy I wanted to know about, it was her and me. That's right, but her and the other guy concern her and me. Even if I only think they do, they do. Did she love the guy, that's what I want to know, or was it, you know, one of those things that happen after a party? And then there's a difference whether it happened, say, before I went up to her place the first time, or after. Well, Christ, I got home in a great mood, as you can imagine. I could feel one of those nights coming on, one of those wonderful, wonderful nights driving around the city. So I've decided to put it all on Austin. Let him absorb the punishment, why should I? I mean, let him earn his keep. Anyway, first let me tell you what happened on the way home. I was crawling along the highway in the late afternoon rush and came to one of those combination exit and entrance ramps that touch the road like an arc. A string of hopeful cars was nudging its way in. You know how it goes. If you're already on the highway and you happen to be in a good mood, you let one car in ahead of you. But if you're not, you stay bumper to bumper with the car in front and say Screw you to the world at large. Well, this big white Cadillac tries to squeeze in, but I just keep inching along. He squeezes, I inch. Finally he stops short. I think I've won. I look at him from the corner of my eye, only the corner, mind you, because the rules of the game demand that you make believe you don't see him. If he catches your eye, you have to let him in. That's the rule. Well, this guy has no sense of the sport, he rolls down his electric window and calls me a crummy kid. I flip into neutral, pull up the brake, turn and look at him full face. He has an imposing jaw, but I'm committed. What did you say, I said. I said you eat shit, he said. Would you like to prove that, I said. Yeah, he said, and the big white door of the big white Cadillac opens up, and out steps a big white man. Was he big! Well, cars are honking, guys leaning out, yelling for us to knock it off. Pull down there, I said, go on, you stupid bastard, pull down there, and I point to the bottom of the exit, where there was a broad shoulder of grass, pull down there and I'll ram your head up your ass. He socked himself into the car, whanged the door shut and lurched down the exit ramp, rolling up on the grass to wait for me. Well, old buddy, this was the moment of truth, traffic had begun to move. Gently I stepped on the clutch, gently I released the brake, gently I slipped into gear, and speedily I continued on my way home. In defense of myself I might say that I believe I was acting in the spirit of enlightened self-interest. Suppose Russia were to do likewise, wouldn't the world be a rosy place. On the other hand—I anticipate you—suppose the United States acted that way, wouldn't the world be a red place. Well, be that as it may, suppose I have slob Austin go back to a former sweetheart. She can have married someone else, someone Austin has never seen. He's still in love with her. He goes to their apartment, knocks on the door. She opens it, dressed in a housecoat. He wants to slip in past her, but she stands in the way. Seeing no one, she closes the door again. He discovers a bottle of milk in front of another door, takes it and places it so that she has to come out into the hallway to get it. He knocks again, and his ruse works. She examines the milk, leaves it there, but in the meantime he gets inside the apartment. There is the husband sitting at the table having breakfast, a round and meaty type which Austin dislikes on sight. She returns from the hall mystified, but the door-knocking has reminded her of Austin. He did that once, she says, after we had a fight. He came back to make up, but before anyone could answer the door he changed his mind and left. She and her husband begin talking about Austin. My mother liked him very much, she says. That's because he was a tribble, the husband says. A tribble? A tribble is a young man with three empty testicles, all mothers like tribbles, they know that their daughters are safe with them. He was very good-looking, she says, but, you know, in all the time I knew him he never once kissed me. Unlike myself, the husband says, and comes around the table, lifts her to her feet and slips off her housecoat. You're insatiable, she says. I was told six months and I intend to make the most of them. We'll have to be careful, she says, and Austin realizes from the talk and the slightly bulging tummy that she's pregnant. He has never seen a pregnant woman so intimately before, and suddenly he knows that she is out of his reach. Before he became invisible, Austin had dreamed of breaking into her apartment and carrying her off right in front of the husband. But now he promises himself that one of the things he'll do after he has settled the world's hash will be to seduce her with his power and wealth. He'll send her expensive presents, flattering letters which will give the next day's news, news that he himself has made. He will overwhelm her with his new abilities. Seeing her here, though, in the arms of her husband he realizes that she genuinely loves him, that he has an outward quality which in fact any woman would like. He may be round and meaty, but he is direct and forceful, not full of fantasy like himself. Well, the husband takes her into the bedroom, not even finishing his bacon and eggs, not even closing the bedroom door. They begin to make love. Austin is torn between staying and leaving and, if he stays, between interrupting the act and enduring it. If he chooses he can easily frighten them out of their senses. He can assault the husband. Tribble indeed, he could make him a nobble. But instead he waits and listens. The sounds of love cover him with loneliness. He puts his fingers in his ears, still the sounds reach him. He wiggles his fingers, filling his head with scratching noises. Then, after a long while, he removes them and listens. The sounds have stopped. He looks into the bedroom, the two of them are lying on their sides facing one another, their bodies uncovered and moist with sweat. The husband's forearm is across her waist, she seems to bend under it, accepting and making room for it. It is a comfort to her. The scene is strangely familiar. Where has he observed it before? And he thinks he remembers his parents once thus when he was an only child. I didn't mean only, I meant tiny. Jesus, do you know I had a brother, a younger brother who died at birth? I haven't thought of him for years. When I was a kid I used to think about him. He would have been two years younger than I. Part of me thought it would have been great if he had lived and been my friend, and part of me was glad that he had died. I haven't thought of that for years. Screw that, screw all that, I'm going to write to Prudence and ask her to marry me. No ifs or buts—she quit her job at MUI to-day—just a simple letter that says Will you marry me. I love you and I want to marry you. I was thinking that Austin would pick up an unfinished piece of bacon from the husband's breakfast plate and sneak away to his next frustration, but, no, he sweeps the plate to the floor and leaves, slamming the door as he goes. No, that's not it either, he crawls into bed on her far side and subtly, insidiously draws her away from the husband. Finally she turns to him and they embrace. Well, maybe. I don't know.

✄ ✄ ✄ ✄ ✄ ✄ ✄ MY STOCK DECLINES at MUI. I bring in tapes, I play one, Fox fidgets, Wally puts on another, Fox goes to the john, Wally gives me a lecture, as follows. I don't hear you talking, kid, I don't hear the slogans, HE WHO LEARNS EARNS, A CHILD TAUGHT IS A FUTURE BOUGHT, HE WHO KNOWS GOES. There's a fucking lot of wisdom in those thoughts, kid. I can't hear nothing, have you got the folder out? I don't hear the pages rattle. You're not doing a social bit here, kid. You can't sit on your can, you got to push. You know what I mean? Push. What's the matter, kid, these guys don't know nothing. If they weren't dopes they'd be selling and you'd be buying. And the dumber they are, the softer they are, that's a basic of salesmanship. I'll tell you something, kid, to a dope I can sell shit in a fancy wrapper. Is that what you're selling me, I said. That's it, kid, be snotty. What do you want, you want to smell them or sell them? I go into a guy's home, if the guy's nice I'm nice, if the guy's snotty I'm snotty. I say to them, Mr. Jerk, I hope you will pardon my expression, but you are a stupid person. Maybe no one ever called you a stupid person before, but I am calling you a stupid person, and I'll tell you why, Mr. Jerk, because I came here in your home to talk about your kid's future, and you're not listening. You listen to the doctor when he comes, don't you? You're shaking your head, Mr. Jerk, does that mean you do or you don't, because I don't know from the way you're acting whether you listen to the doctor. I wouldn't be surprised if you put cotton in your ears and it goes in one ear and out the other, because I came here to tell you something just as important as the doctor. I came here to tell you that if your kid isn't educated he's through. I don't know what your line is, you didn't have the courtesy to acknowledge what your line is, maybe you collect garbage, but I'll tell you something, if your kid doesn't have an education today he won't even collect garbage. You know what he'll do, and I choose my words with full appreciation, he'll be a bum. You feed your kid, don't you, Mr. Jerk? You see to it that he gets nourished right up to the teeth. But what do you do about the mind, because if you don't fill up the mind you might as well throw away all the good nourishment and send him out on the street with the rest of the bums, because that's where he'll end up, standing around on the street with his hands in his pocket. You see these kids with their hands in their pockets, what's on their minds, Mr. Jerk? Who knows, you know what I mean, Mr. Jerk. You see what I'm doing, kid, I get my hooks in and they listen. You're just wasting everybody's time, most of all your own, with this banana-cake shit. Get with it, kid. The banana-cake shit referred to one of the tapes Fox walked out on. Sweet people, the guy about thirty, two children, one eight and the other preschool. And he was no dope

either, he was a color-reproduction expert for an adver-
tising agency. Anyway when we came to FAMILY IS
FUTURE he told me that his worst day since he got
married was better than the best day before he got married, which sounds wild, but not if you saw his little
round wife with her black hair parted in the middle and
pulled back in a bun behind her head, and the two kids,
quiet without being stiff. Then he told me about the
banana cake. It seems that when he was a child in North
Carolina banana cake was his favorite food, but he hadn't
had any in so long he had forgotten about it. Then one
night—after he and his wife had been married five years
—he came home and she had baked a banana cake. Five
years, she never knew he liked banana cake, he didn't
know she could bake it, which I gather not everybody
can do. Well, Fox walked out at this part, and Wally
turned the tape off, but the guy had gone on to explain
that the banana cake had made him so happy he couldn't
get to sleep that night. He was afraid it would all be
taken away from him, wife, kids, home, job. It wasn't,
however, and they invited me back the next evening,
when the wife would have a banana cake prepared. I
didn't go, but I'm sure it was great banana cake. I knew
Fox wouldn't learn anything about selling books from
the tape, I just thought it would be good to listen to.
So what are we going to do? There are eaters of banana
cake, there are Foxes and Wallys, and right in the middle there is me, which is the worst position of all, I suspect. Not that everybody I do for MUI eats banana cake.
For instance, there is the carnivorous Mrs. Frank, more

about whom in a minute. Or there is the newsstand dealer who twenty years ago, when he was on furlough from the army, met a famous American philosopher. The philosopher saw in the young soldier a Natural Philosopher. He even wrote an article about the soldier to prove it. Well, this naturally philosophic soldier never got over it. For twenty years he's been going around believing that he is the repository of special wisdom. He writes letters to magazines and world leaders and even claims to be amused that a man of his qualities is running a newsstand. I don't think his wife is, however. Then there was another guy who works in a commercial darkroom, where the chemical fumes are so intense he can't smell or taste food any more. Leaning over a table lamp he showed me the scar tissue instead of mucous membrane inside his nose, and also took out a pair of his work pants from which the chemicals had eaten away the cuffs. He did all this with a smile. Before I left we went into his bedroom so that I could see how the fire escape was rusted away. Anyone trying to use it would fall to the street. All smiling. Then there was a big meaty housewife, who in every sentence used the word frig, pronouncing it mincingly to let me know she knew it stood for fuck, which she refrained from saying out of delicacy. This woman's husband told me that when he first saw her she was working in a candy store, the owner's daughter. Before he had spoken to her, just having seen her over the counter and through the store window, he told his buddies that she was the girl he was going to marry. None of them believed me, he said, not one of them thought I could. But I did. Fox had absolutely no comment when I ran this one, and I felt as if I had told a dirty joke to a bunch of nuns. Then there was a woman whose midget uncle one night had brought Tallulah Bankhead home, where she sat with the family till two A.M. I didn't know what this meant or was intended to mean, except that the woman spoke of it in a way that made me think it was the first autobiographical revelation she made to strangers. Also there was a kid who spat on one of my foldouts. The father, a psychologist, asked me if I didn't think the boy was wonderfully aggressive. I said if he was my kid I'd bash his skull in, so that before I left, the father called me a Nazi brute. Well, if these encounters amuse you they're not a complete loss, that's what I say. But after twenty or thirty interviews you begin to realize something, that you're using up people's time, stealing it in fact. Most of them work hard all day, come home and want to watch television or hop into bed and screw or sit around and drink, and here I arrive, fake my way into their living rooms with my big black presentation folder and my little invisible tape recorder, and I steal their precious time. Then I turn their foolishness over to my master, who will make from it a poison formula to lay them out on the order pad some day. That isn't nice, is it? So if I goof, if I just let them talk about themselves and if what they say is useless to Fox and Wally, well then, bravo for me. Let them get another boy-spy, which I suppose they'll be doing soon enough. Mrs. Frank, mentioned above, is a special case, like the psychologist, not in our test block of five-story tenements. She and her plump silent son live around the corner from me, one of the families Mr. Goldhammer recommended. No doorbell ringing here, all was accomplished in genteel and professional fashion. I phoned for the appointment. Yes, Mr. Goldhammer had spoken to her about me, said I was a very interesting young man doing important work for the country. Come over whenever you like, just call beforehand, she said. No fun at all, I thought, no danger, no resistance. Well, there was fun. The moment, the second, the millisecond I saw her I knew that Mrs. Frank was more organ than person. Wet. Her lips shone, the lower rims of her eyes glistened, her tiny hand was warmly damp. For a while—until she made up her mind about me, I guess—she was all eyes. I thought she would lick me. Well, we raced that interview, Mrs. Frank nodding, nodding, Junior saying nothing, only looking, looking with the mother's same wet eyes. Then—so Mommie and the man could talk—Junior was put to bed. Every five minutes for half an hour she checked him, and when she finally announced that he was asleep we ourselves were in bed before five minutes more had passed. It was a strange seduction, no seduction at all. She had so shown the wetness, or whatever the quality was, that nothing had to be said. As she came out of Junior's room for the last time, I stood up, kissed her, and she led me away. I won't tell you how many times the dirty deed was done that night. You'd think I was bragging, and although I've heard of similar exploits by others, I never thought I'd be the hero of one myself. Let me here repeat a familiar sentiment: a man is only so good as the woman he's with. Mrs. Frank is very good. The night was like a week to me. I napped between, deep dreamless naps, waking in surprise, then we'd sit at different ends of her great bed, talking and kidding around, tickling one another's feet, and a funny thing struck me, how much this was like children in a sandbox. Bed is the adult's playground. It seems sort of regressive when you think of it, but it really is the only place you can giggle easily when you're grown up. In a way, though, it was too much. Not that it wasn't fun, because she's a small and charming creature, a little worn about the tit and tummy, but pretty and golden, and it was fun. She had to tell me, however, the gory story of her marriage, some years dissolved, to what she claims was an unconscious fag. Every time he came near me for sex, she said, it looked like there was someone behind pushing him. Well, I guess she ought to know. But I think she still loves the guy. In the midst of the tossing and turning she called me by his name. And then I couldn't get out of my mind a picture of the plump silent boy in the other room. He was the adult and we were the children. It didn't seem fair. Well, whether on his account, Mrs. Frank's account, Mr. Frank's account, or my own, after I left, which was about five A.M., I was overcome by a depression. If all animals are sad after intercourse, I was five times sad, and on my way home, no one around, I walked into a traffic light. Later I realized that I had seen the light and walked into it anyway. I like Mrs. Frank all right, but I guess I don't approve of her. I might if the boy hadn't been there, but as it was, the night made me feel like an accomplice, or one of many accomplices, in the bad thing she was doing to him. Don't ask me what bad thing, I don't know, but when I got home I couldn't sleep, so I wrote about my pal Austin, which writing I will send you under separate cover, in a plain wrapper.

✳ ✳ ✳ ✳ ✳ ✳ ✳ ✳ ✳ FIRST LET ME tell you about Austin, then Prudence. (I got an answer, from Italy! She accepted.) But Austin, poor Austin. He's decided to commit himself, informally, to a nuthouse. In a nuthouse he will be safe. If a patient detects and reports him, the patient won't be believed. Also in a nuthouse Austin can indulge in some much-needed—you should pardon the expression—social intercourse. Besides staff quarters there are three main buildings at the nuthouse, Administration, Men's, and Women's. Which will Austin pick? Is it a question? Which would you pick, old man, if you suffered from—or, let's say, were graced by—Austin's condition. Exactly. And the accommodations there were decorous, considering the function they performed. Each patient had her own room. As he ascended the five floors, Austin noticed that the inmates became more bizarre and their appointments more prison-like. The bottom floor looked like the YWCA, whereas on the top floor the windows were barred and the walls padded. There were about one hundred and fifty patients in all, and it was on the third floor—in the middle of the madness, so to speak—that Austin found a friend. She was Greek, he decided, because of her large dark eyes and olive skin and black hair and, O yes, because on the door of her room was a name card reading Electra Papas. What an evocative combination of the classic and the modern! Electra Papas, a name to conjure incest as well as fried clams and apple pie. The instant he saw her he knew that she was special, because, although her back was toward him and she was combing her long black hair in front of a mirror, she was naked. On the first floor you would not see such innocent abandon. Nor on the fifth, where ladies given to disrobing were encased in buttonless smocks sewed securely twixt the nether limbs. Only on the third, the mediocritas aurea, might one find an Electra Papas languidly combing her dark locks naked. Needless to say, Austin stood in the doorway entranced. Shortly, however, a nurse passing by looked in and tsked her tongue at Electra. Like any good obedient third-floor patient Electra scurried to the bed, where her clothes were neatly folded. On they went, while the indulgent nurse stood smiling, shaking her head in amusement. When the last button was buttoned, the nurse nodded approvingly and went her way. Immediately Electra removed her clothes and returned to comb and mirror. She seemed to be humming some strange exotic tune as she stroked her hair. Austin listened. Ah, it was an off-key rendition of I'm in the Mood for Love. He was ravished. Stealthily he crept up behind her. She feels his body heat on her bare back. Without turning, but peering into the mirror, she says, Henry, is that you? Henry, Henry, where have you been? Henry, are you going to stand there like a fool, or are you going to bend over like a nice man and bite me on the shoulder? She pointed with her right hand to a spot on her left shoulder. Austin bent over, bit, was suffused with pleasure, and came. I don't know if I should make him come here or not. What do you think? It's just that it's such a yummy situation, and it would be unreasonable to expect him to perform at length and with assurance first crack in the sack. I mean, isn't it better for him to throw one away and start with a clean slate? All right, he comes. Now I was thinking of a comic bit here where after coming on her bare back he scurries around for a towel as if he had spilt tea on the couch. It would screw the mood, though, wouldn't it? Yeah, so just in time he swivels to one side and ejaculates out the open window. An image of thousands of his selves falling three stories to the grounds of an insane asylum flashes through his head. He is oddly pleased. She turns around and rises, puts her arms about his neck. Henry, Henry, she says. He eases her over to the bed and lays her down. Instantly she is ready, she is precooked. Once he lays her, twice, thrice, fource. Henry, she says, Henry, ooo, ah-h-h, oh-h-h, Henry-y-y-y-y. Comes? She comes and comes. Wildly. Her appreciation is so vocal that the nurse returns. Electra, the nurse shouts, seeing the patient spread-eagle on the bed, which, by the way, is wet with enthusiasm. Austin tumbles off, moves out of harm's way. Electra clutches hungrily at the air. Doctor, doctor, the nurse calls. Running footsteps, and a young white-frocked male, stethoscope hanging limply from his jacket pocket, appears in the doorway. Anxiously he looks from nurse to patient, while Austin views the scene dispassionately. Although the young doctor means business, the nurse can see in the subtle involuntary movement of his eyes that the business is only ninety-nine per cent medicine, because here on the bed is Electra Papas moaning for her fled lover. O, she is saying, O Henry, Henry, Henry. Austin observes a rare reversal of roles. The nurse takes charge, she is one hundred per cent medicine. She needs the doctor's help to bring Miss Papas out of sexual hysteria, she also must guard Miss Papas, and the doctor too, from the forces of nature. Luckily Electra is squirming so that the nurse has no difficulty extracting a sheet from beneath her and covering her with it. Frantically Electra undulates beneath the sheet. Well, finally the doctor pulls himself together—isn't that a great phrase, it means releasing the superego to extinguish the id—and says Restrain her, nurse, I'll get a syringe. The doctor disappears. Running footsteps down the hall. Soon he is back, ejaculates a cc or two of colorless liquid into the air to guard against air bubbles and plunges the easing tool into the lady's, of all places, arm. Electra's writhings lessen, there is a final jerk, a final sighing moan, and peace overcomes her. Once again the doctor pulls himself together. You'll take care of her, nurse, the doctor says authoritatively. Of course, doctor. I'll be in my office, if you need me, nurse. Yes, doctor. And Austin watches as the nurse uncovers Electra, corpse-like now, wets a cloth and wipes the sweat or whatever from Electra's thighs. The nurse shakes her head in wonderment at the ingenuity of the female body, which in the intensity of its delusion apparently can generate a sperm-like substance. She even rubs a bit between her fingers, marveling. Hey, man, how about that? We gonna sell that to the Reader's Digest Book Club? And I've got an idea for the next chapter even wilder. In the Men's Building. Watch out. The letter from Prudence said: I am in Italy answering some questions for myself, not the ones I was brought here to answer, but some. Mother apparently thought that here I could make a better decision about having the baby. I didn't tell her, but I want you to know that I made up my mind before your letter arrived. In fact I made it up before I left the States. I made up my mind the moment I found out. I will have the baby, of course. I don't think it really cares about the circumstances of its conception, and since I've always tried to honor the feelings of others in the small details of living I will continue to honor them in the fact of living. That's the Catholic viewpoint humanly reduced, isn't it? Well, as I told you, Rome has large wisdoms for a Protestant like me. I don't really know why Mother brought me to Italy to make up my mind. She hasn't shown me her own feelings about having the baby. Maybe she doesn't have any. I suspect she doesn't and that she merely wants me to be in a place where human beings are most themselves, so that I won't be pushed to a decision by the influences that operate in one's own territory. France or Spain or England would have done as well, I think. But maybe Italy is special. First of all, there's the sun, which rules everything. Since we've been here it has rained only once, and then torrentially on an afternoon at four o'clock. After half an hour it stopped, as if God, knowing that the land needed water, provided it as quickly as possibly so as not to disturb anyone's vacation. By evening the streets were dry and we went to the Baths of Caracalla to hear an off-season production of Tosca. I giggled through the whole first act and embarrassed Mother and my sister Billy, who took the thing so seriously. I love Rome. I've been to Milan and Venice and Florence, and south as far as Naples, but nothing compares to Rome. Mother found a wonderful hotel this time. I've met only one American here, an intense and anti-American young American who keeps telling me about the important work he is doing back in the States on Heidegger and how the Thomists in the college where he teaches are trying to get him fired because of it. He's a former divinity student with the most attractive scar on his cheek, which he keeps rubbing, and I think he's sweet on me. Little does he know what evil lurks in the thommies of women. About your letter. I hope you called my house and learned from my aunt—who is the lady you spoke to, if you spoke to anyone—that I had left the country. I wouldn't want you to think I had received and not answered your letter. It was such a short letter. Here, where people talk about the least important things at great length, it sounded compulsive. Will I marry you? Yes, I will. Perhaps. But I'm like the Italians, I must talk. So you must listen to my long answer to your short question. Yes, I will marry you, my dear. But I am going to have this baby, and if you marry me you will have to be its father. It will be a human being who will need a father, just as I am a woman and need a husband. I know that you are a loving person and that you credit life, otherwise I could not think of marrying you. But I know, too, that you have special needs that sometimes work against your lovingness. I don't know how demanding these needs are for you, and you don't either, I suspect. So if you marry me we will both be taking a chance on them. I am willing to take that chance, but I want you to consider it before you take it. If we marry I want to have another child as soon as possible, so that even by mechanical standards you will know that I belong to you as much as to anyone else. One wife and two children make quite a different purchase from me alone on Sunday afternoon by the river. Do you understand me, my dear? If you marry me you will be doing a very grownup thing. I know you are hard-working, sincere and able, but much of the play will be gone from your life. You used to tell me about your long summers at the beach, how your mother would bring you orange juice in bed and you would get up and eat a soft-boiled egg and go to the store for her, and that would be your only duty of the day. Then you would call for your friends and swim. If the east wind blew, the water would be calm and cool. If the west wind blew, it would be warm and rough. And you would swim until you shivered, then run to your house and change your bathing suit, call again for your friends, walk along the beach, play word games, take one more dip before lunch. You told me how your mother warmed your milk and put a teaspoon of sugar into it. In the afternoon you'd play ball on the beach, swimming when you wanted, not bothering to change now because all your suits were wet. Then after dinner you would gather again, boys and girls, to play hide-and-seek until it was dark, resisting the last call of the day when your mother or father would come to get you. Then, in pajamas you would ask for a piece of bread to take to bed. Suddenly it was another day, the sun blazing again, your father already off to the city, and the whole game began over. Because you told me about those days with such feeling I've remembered them, and I wonder if you've had your fill. They're still yours, you know, for a few years anyway, if you want and need them badly. But if you marry me they will be over. The child I have in me and the child you may get in me will be the ones to play on the beach, not you. That's the letter, man. Like a slob I cried when I read about myself as a boy. Jesus, I'm crying now. I don't know what to say to her, I don't know what I want.

✖ ✖ ✖ ✖ ✖ ✖ ✖ ✖ MADNESS TO COME
between a man and his madness. Around eight o'clock,
after it got dark, I noticed Jose from my window walking up and down in front of the building. I guessed it
had to do with his cousin across the street because every
time he got to the corner he'd turn, stop and stare at
the nuns' house. I watched him and until a police car
came cruising by, slower than they usually cruise, I had
no intention of interfering. And, sure enough, by the
time I got downstairs it had rounded the block and was
cruising by again, even slower. I told him that those
cops were looking him over. They have reason, he said,
they smell my violence. He really looked wild. He was
dressed OK, but there was a tension in his neck and legs,
and his head was thrust forward like an angry nut. I am
about to violate that sanctuary of virginity, he said, the
blood of my blood is being held prisoner, I must release
her. You mean your cousin? Today she promised to come
to me and she has not. When did she promise? This
morning. She actually promised, to do what? To come
to me. You mean up to your room? Yes, to my room.
Well, maybe she changed her mind, how do you know
she's a prisoner? Because she promised to come. Well,
anything could have happened, maybe she couldn't make

it or something. Of course she couldn't make it, and this is why I will tear down the door of those malevolent penguins. No, I mean maybe she tried to sneak out, and it wasn't possible. Sneak, she said she would come and she would not sneak, she would come rending her veil in two. Well, maybe she would and maybe she wouldn't, I don't see how you know. I know because she has Llano blood, are you questioning the blood of my family? I'm only questioning your grasp of the facts, Jose. Come on upstairs, we'll have a drink, and we can talk it over. No, if she escapes and I am not here she will go back. Why would she go back, who's questioning the blood of your family now? She knows where you live, doesn't she, I mean the room and everything. I have described it to her a hundred times. Well, if she does get out she can certainly walk across the street by herself, can't she? And if she doesn't, you'll learn all about it in the morning. Tomorrow she will be gone. Where? They will have sent her away. Away where? My friend, he said, you do not know the resources of Mother Church. They have secluded retreats where they send the troublesome religious, whom they call insane. O come on, Jose, for Chrissake, you're thinking of the Spanish Inquisition, that parish is run by simple-minded Irishmen. They will smuggle her into Red China, she will be lost to me forever. Well, they're not going to do it tonight, and if you stay here you're sure as hell going to be picked up by those cops. The nuns probably saw you glaring at them from over here and thought you were some kind of madman, which I'm not sure you aren't. You think that? No, not really, Jose, but I was watching you from upstairs and I could see why somebody might, so why not come upstairs and we'll talk about it. We'll both watch from the window, and if the door opens you can run down and grab her, I'll even help you. He shook his head. She will be gone in the morning, he said. The squad car came around the block again, and without another word he came up to my room. At first he insisted on standing by the window, but after a couple of drinks he sat down and told me the story. It seems that that morning he had threatened to expose their relationship—such as it is— if she didn't come with him immediately, and after much badgering she promised to meet him in his room when her classes were done at three o'clock. Well, that's why she hasn't come, I said, you forced the promise out of her. A promise is a promise, he said, at least to a Spaniard. You don't seem to realize that you've put the girl in an impossible position. I, he said, I, she has put herself in the impossible position, I will extricate her from it. Do you actually think you're going to solve this girl's problems and your own by getting her into your room and into bed? He spat his spitless spit. Do you think I am interested in a cheap seduction, the quick answer of the flesh? I have written a Very Tale for her, which will show her the question and the answer, the problem and the solution, the dilemma and the choice. What, about a nun with a priest on her back, I said, and I wasn't far wrong. So he read me his wildness, which I transcribe more or less from memory. Bear with it, there's an epilogue. Once upon a time there was a young nun who liked to walk about the ample convent grounds observing the beauties of nature. In every cloud and blade of grass she saw some aspect of God's grandeur. One summer's day, while strolling along the banks of the stream that ran through the convent property, she decided to sit down and rest a moment. It was very warm, and the sight of the trees overhead, the chirping of the birds and the sound of the rushing waters were so pleasant that she fell asleep. It so happened that two beavers were swimming downstream looking for a place to build a lodge and a dam, and when they reached the nun lying asleep on the bank the male beaver beat his broad tail on the water to draw his companion's attention to the strange sight. They had never seen a nun before. So they swam to the bank and examined her from head to foot, much marveling. This must be some rare natural formation, they thought. The nun, being by temperament innocent and trusting, was sleeping with her legs apart, and the beavers ambled between them, enjoying the shade of her dark long habit. Deep under her skirts the beavers discovered what they thought was an abandoned burrow, and cautiously they entered the moist opening. They were very pleased. Here, they decided, is a fine place to live, here we shall build a dam to hold the waters after rain, and here we shall bring up our young. Immediately they set about carrying branches, mud, and stones from the banks of the stream, and before long they had finished their dam. They then decided that before the sun went down they would make a foray into the woods to gather birch and aspen bark for supper. While they were gone, however, the nun awoke and returned to the convent unaware that she took with her the beavers' home. That evening after prayers and supper, when she went to pee, she found she could not. Nor could she the following morning. Nor after the midday repast. Nor even after supper the second night. At first she thought it only a temporary indisposition, but when a week had gone by, she found herself in severe distress, not only because of the physical discomfort but also because her figure was changing. She had become plainly round about the middle. The other nuns, jealous of her reputation for piety, began to spread nasty rumors, and when they reached the ears of the mother superior she called the young nun to her and bluntly asked if she had dallied with the gardner or the chaplain. The nun swore that she had not, and although the mother superior believed her she instructed the old physician who attended the community to examine her. Virgo intacta, the physician reported. Immediately there were hopes of a virgin birth, which the doctor blasted by adding that the young nun was suffering from a mysterious impaction which would have to be removed if she was to remain in good health. Specialists were brought from the most distant regions of the land, and although each of them had his own solution to the problem none was successful. It was finally decided that someone, both able and trustworthy, would have to proceed to the seat of the trouble to remove the impaction. There were a number of volunteers, among them some nuns of mannish mode as well as quite a few priests of dubious virtue, but no religious was found able, experienced and agile enough to perform the sensitive mission. All this time the nun was growing larger and larger. Finally, in the army, of all places, a soldier was discovered who had served with distinction in the recent war as a demolitions expert. He was tall and dark and a youth of unquestioned purity. The day of the mission, which came to be known as Operation Operation, arrived, and the young hero, equipped with web-feet, skin-tight plastic clothing, and a large supply of oxygen, was brought to the convent. Both his mother and father, as well as a special delegation of church dignitaries from Rome, were on hand to see him off. It was a solemn occasion. Rumors had persisted, so that not only the health of the nun but the reputation of the entire order was at stake. Dynamite strapped to his legs, crowbar and hand grenades attached to his belt, the young soldier set forth. A day and a night he was gone. Finally after twenty-six hours there was a muffled boom from the nun's lower regions and then a great rush of waters. Swept out were the ruins of the beavers' dam and the soldier himself. The nun heaved a great sigh of relief, as did the mother superior, the delegation from Rome, and in fact the entire nation. Despite the clamor for a public appearance, the young man was spirited away to a secret meeting of the Church dignitaries and closely questioned about his feat. There he confessed that at one point, wearied by his long journey, he had been overcome by lassitude, lain down, gone to sleep and dreamed. In the dream, he explained, he had met the nun on a more equal footing and fallen in love with her. The

136   *charles simmons*

dignitaries were shocked. Exactly what had ensued in the dream, they wanted to know. The young soldier blushed scarlet. Quickly his plastic suit was examined, and it was determined that he had experienced while asleep a nocturnal emission. Thus it was decided after long debate that the nun would have to be released from her vows and marry the young man. She was not at all displeased with the outcome of events, and although in this way she lost sainthood she gained womanhood. You understand the symbolism, Jose asked. Nothing could be clearer, I said, and suddenly I was sick of Jose and his sick little Very Tales and his screwy plans to seduce his nun-cousin. For all I knew there wasn't even any Rita-Sister Barbara in the school across the street. But he persisted. Who are the beavers, he asked. O come on, Jose. You see what a brilliant metaphorical rendering it is. Rendering of what, I said. Of her situation, he said. It sounds more like a rendering of your situation. I am the soldier, he said. Well, you may be the soldier, but how come the nun keeps changing sizes, at one point she's small enough to be your bride and at another she's big enough to be, you should pardon the expression, your mother. Wow, talk about the wrong thing to say! I thought you had eluded them, he said. Eluded who? The Jews, he said, I thought that unlike the rest of your countrymen you had seen through their devices. What are you talking about? I thought you understood that psychoanalysis was at the center of the Jewish conspiracy to strip us of our manhood. Look, Jose, that was an amusing story, sort of, but it came out of your head and because of that I'm sure it has much more to do with you than with a nun who you claim is your cousin, who you claim loves you, and who you claim promised to meet you today. Does anyone have to be a psychoanalyst to see you have all sorts of Oedipal things working for you in that story, and anyway why get so excited about it? He held up his hand and said May I ask you a question? Shoot. You have told me many times about your Catholic background, you even entertained a priest in this room, but really you are a Jew, aren't you? Is that another metaphorical rendering? No, you are a Jew, aren't you? I could tell from his face that he meant it, and as I considered what to say I learned something rather important about myself. On the one hand I was furious that he was about to launch again into his familiar anti-semitic line. On the other hand I was furious at being asked whether I was a Jew. I never thought I was anti-semitic, but apparently I am. I say this with a kind of wonder. Well, there wasn't much more. He left with the question unanswered. By me, that is, which I guess was answer enough for him. You know, plenty of friends in my life have faded away. But this is the first one who died.

❈ ❈ ❈ ❈ ❈ ❈ ❈ ❈ TODAY I SHOWED up at MUI with a Negro family so proper and carefully spoken and responsive that I thought at last I had a tape which both pleased me and would be useful to Fox. In none of our sales-technique conferences had there been any discussion of Negroes, and all this MUI shit about educating the children, making a better world, and the importance of books this family agreed with entirely. What I mean is that the Negro's naivete may just be old-fashioned effective faith. Well, I never got to play it. Fox called me into his office and told me he had decided I was a writer after all. At first he had doubted it, he had heard too many young men say they wanted to be writers, but I was different, and it would be better for me if I got down to business. Christ, the way he spoke, I thought he was going to stake me to a private fellowship. But then he started shifting papers on his desk, like I should go already, and I realized I was being canned. I never really thought I would be, you know. Anyway, I said Mr. Fox, how do you know I'm a writer when you never read anything I wrote? I read those fake articles. But you had read them when you first hired me as Wally's assistant, I said. I wasn't paying attention then. Are you firing me, I said. I'm advising you. Mr.

Fox, may I take back something I once said to you? Was it good or bad, what you said? Bad. Take it back. You don't have a goyische kopf at all. You see, he said, we were both wrong. And that was that. Well, Harvey called me up about five o'clock. I told him the news and he asked me to join him and Mrs. Fox for dinner at a restaurant. When I arrived they were sitting close around one corner of the table like a fashionable mother-and-son team. The last time I had seen them together, at the unwedding, they had not looked fashionable. But now there was a glint of Oriental mockery in Lady Fox's eye and an amused reaction in his. I was amazed by the body of their common understandings, mutual acquaintances, the small details of living they could refer to with confidence. They seemed to have been absorbed into one another's worlds—he into hers more than she into his—but it was quite an extension of their activities since the covert screwing in MUI's top-floor apartment. Everything went well until Lady F began discussing literature. Eugene O'Neill, she said, was in her opinion the greatest playwright America had ever produced. This raised something sharp in Harvey. He folded his napkin, put it beside his plate, and said When I hear O'Neill thus praised I think of Andre Gide's remark when asked who the greatest French poet of the nineteenth century was. He said Victor Hugo—unfortunately. I believe Paul Valery made that remark, Mrs. Fox said. I was surprised she could distinguish Valery from Herbert Hoover. Not Harvey, however. Must you perpetuate the mistake made by that clown in Esquire? I didn't know what Harvey was talking about, but apparently Mrs. Fox did, so she began talking about Loretta Young and how it was undoubtedly some inner quality that kept her youthful. Harvey said that on the contrary he had heard it was because she wore a Loretta Young mask. After a few more exchanges, all of which Mrs. Fox took in good grace, she announced that she had to join her daughter and her daughter's girlfriend at the theater. Toujour la jeunesse pour rich Mrs. Fox, and as she left us to our dessert I half expected her to give Harvey money for the check, as a mommie might. But we rose, I shook Mrs. Fox's hand, wrinkled but not veiny, brown but manicured, and Harvey smiled, even bent in a modified Continental bow. How would he come on with me now that mommie was gone? Had he been squared off, would he play it cozy? No, he came on salty. You no doubt wonder why I have gathered you here, he said—well, no reason, pal, it's a gesture. You're helping me celebrate my release from MUI. That's it, he said, and went on to tell me that he was living at home, where as far as his parents were concerned he was still collaborating on the musical comedy, which got him out of the house two or three nights a week. Lady F, which is his term for her by the way, had sublet a friend's apartment. It was very elegant, Harvey said, and he was slowly moving more and more of his clean shirts there. I know Harvey's parents pretty well, especially his mother, who always struck me as discerning and discreet. Do they buy the musical-comedy bit, I asked. You mean really, who knows? My guess is they figure I have some chick on the hook. What would they think if they knew it was Mrs. Fox, I said. It was a gross question. The same thing you think, what do you think? How do you mean? I mean what do you think of Selma Fox? In what way, I said. Come on, pal, level with me. I didn't know what to say, I felt as he must have felt when Mr. Fox invited him to marry her. So I said Jesus, Harvey, I don't think anything about her. I guess I just see a kind of symbiosis working, and I'm for both parts of that word, I'm for the sym and I'm for the bio. He considered that for a while, and as he considered I asked him, by the way, what he thought of Mary. I like her, I actually like her, OK? OK, I said, and I like Mrs. Fox, and that ended it for the moment. He went on to tell me about the job Mrs. Fox had gotten him, which may account for his sharpness when she started talking about literature. It seems he's teaching poetry to a Barry Feldshuh, former —ain't names grand—shoe manufacturer. Mr. Feldshuh is not a beginner, Harvey explained. Before Harvey he studied poetry with a guy who since got an appointment as poet-in-residence at a California college. Who says rhyme doesn't pay? So Harvey's doing the job now, for which he receives one hundred (100) dollars per lesson. How long do the lessons last? Two or three hours, Harvey said. Is the guy queer or something? Very ascetic, Harvey said, eats figs and nuts, considers himself a sacred vessel. But how does somebody teach poetry? I read him a poem and we discuss it. That's all, don't you answer his correspondence or catalogue his library or something? Well, he said—and this was the poop—we also spend some of each lesson working over his own poems. What kind of poems? Poems, poems, they're difficult to describe, and he pulled out a paper on which was a ten-line composition about a pigeon pecking at frozen vomit on New Year's Day, which image was likened to a toothless infant negotiating a frozen Milkyway, which image led to a description of the baby soiling himself. You're supposed to work this over, I asked. I've already worked it over. And for this you get one hundred (100) dollars? For this and the discussion of a classic poem, Harvey said, but there's something that worries me, my predecessor had connections and could get the stuff published. Maybe he fee-split with the editors, I suggested for a joke. I've been thinking about that, Harvey said. Otherwise Mr. Feldshuh says I'm great, much better than the other guy. You don't have to call him Mister with me, I said, which Harvey ignored. Last week I gave him a fringe benefit, I translated one of his poems into Latin. I told him that in a thousand years the English language would have changed so that the meaning of his work would be available only to a few scholars but that Latin would always be understood by literate readers. Does Mr. Feldshuh understand Latin, I asked. Are you kidding? Anyway, Mr. Feldshuh was so pleased with the translation that he had it inscribed on parchment and set behind glass, and he's commissioned me to translate all his poems—at one hundred (100) dollars a poem. Do you know Latin that well, I asked, suppose he shows your translations to a classics scholar? I thought of that, Harvey said, but no one can tell what the English means in the first place. I've got this thing wrapped up, I just have to establish myself with the magazine editors. Book editors are no problem, Harvey explained, we just go to one of the marginal houses and offer to underwrite cost plus a reasonable profit. He's had two books published already. Ah, but this wasn't all. It seems that under the regime of Harvey's predecessor, every time Feldshuh secreted ten poems or so they would be sent off to an eminent—and I mean eminent—critic for comment, along with a certified check for five hundred (500) dollars. A covering letter would explain that Feldshuh was a rich man who loved poetry and wanted the eminent critic's eminent criticism. The critic was exhorted to be perfectly candid, since the money was his whether he approved of the poems or not. The gimmick, it seems, was that if the critic praised he got another batch and another check. If he panned, the five hundred (500) was it. Harvey had with him one such reply from an eminent critic, which went like this. In my opinion these are extraordinary poems. If they are primarily poems for the unconscious, as perhaps all poems should be, their surface is for the eye and ear. You say that these poems came to you automatically, sometimes in dreams. Yeats said that in dreams responsibility begins. One might add that perhaps it ends there too. When the impulse to be known can travel from the core of one man, through his mind and hand, back through the eye and mind of another man, into his very core, this is art. I particularly admire your fearlessness in using commonplace objects as host to your uncommon metaphorical conceptions, as in the poem beginning Five prongs has my fork. I also admire your great daring in the face of complexity. You have not shirked the poet's absolute duty to demand of the reader all his perceptive skills. You are not afraid of rejection, thus you will be accepted. I find in your work, at least as much of it as I have seen (dig?), a startling parallel to so-called action painting. Although your poems are charged with feeling, their true subject is poetry—poetry itself. You write poems about poetry, just as these painters, as I understand their work, paint paintings about painting, using their emotions as a medium of comment. Finally let me say that your evocation of the massive symbolic charge in the everyday contents of the kitchen drawer is one of the masterful technical accomplishments in recent poetry. Cookthings is a thing of stature. And then this whore quotes the whole poem back at Feldshuh. Potatoe masher,/ Press yourself/ Boldly against/ The unheld, unholding/ Cool pot holder./ Tin cup/ Bent for discard/ Be beggared and jingle,/ And opener/ How many cans/ Can you have had?/ As many as the spatula,/ Flapper,/ Egger-on of near-chicks/ In heat?/ O nutcracker,/ Crush/ The knife sharpener/ As a first move/ Toward peace. And here's the crease, man, these five-C criticisms are not solely for Feldshuh's immediate ego gratification. Three things are done with them. The two longest and most appreciative were used as introductions to Feldshuh's two books. Others were excerpted to reproduce on the jackets. And others—get this—were placed in fancy magazines as book reviews. Now, how was all this last accomplished? The mind boggles. The critics chosen for the introductions were approached with a we-know-you-were-honest letter, and since a publisher seems willing to take a chance on these poems, would it be all right if we used, etc.? Another five Cs was offered, natch. To the jacket blurbers, an additional one C apiece. As to the book reviews, Harvey's predecessor would go to the editor of an otherwise honest journal and announce that such-and-such an eminent critic has evinced interest in Feldshuh's poetry and would like to review it. The eminent critic is so eminent that the editor is glad to use anything he writes. Then teacher goes back to the eminent critic and says that such-and-such an editor would like the critic to review Feldshuh's book, would the eminent critic consent to having his previous honest comments on the poetry appear as a review? There's another two Cs forthcoming, particularly since the august journal dispenses only honorariums for reviewing. Well, with a minority of abstentions and a majority of accessions, Feldshuh's reputation has been solidly established in the literary world. I don't know what you have to worry about then, I said. I guess there was an edge to my tone because he said This is no snap job, you know, I may only spend three hours a week with the guy, but I do a lot of preparation, and I work my ass off on the Latin translations. You can't have it both ways, I said, either it's a good job or it's a shitty job, which is it? You aren't jealous, are you, pal? When I see a plump rich whore walking in her finery, am I jealous? Sure I am, I always wanted to be a whore. Let's stuff that, pal, would you take the job if it was offered to you? Of course I would, I'm unemployed, and any time you want to ask me out to join you and your ladyfriend for a free meal, call me up, I'm always available. And if this rubs you the wrong way, let me explain myself. When you were captured by Lady Fox's crazy good screwing I had nothing or little to say, because who am I to question the direction a cock points, but easy money is something else again. Especially when you don't have access to any, isn't that right, pal? I got fired from MUI because I was resisting these vain manipulators, these Foxy Feldshuhs and felt-shoed Foxes, I resisted them because they don't daddy the world as the world should be daddied. As far as I'm concerned, they would capture us and feed on our tender parts. And I'll tell you something, I'll outlast them, I'll see them die without the prize. I'll get the prize, even Jose will get the prize, but you won't, Harvey, not if you suck at the groin of easy money. Screw the bladder out of Mrs. Fox, she's yours to enjoy. Even sell your heart, that's what it's for, but for Chrissake keep your head for yourself. And don't call me pal again, because I'm neither your pal nor your peer. You're beneath me. No letter from you, man.

❋ ❋ ❋ ❋ ❋ ❋ ❋ SINCE YOU HAVEN'T written, I won't give you news, I'll answer a question you asked a month ago. Is Austin tragic or comic? He's neither. The tragic hero says this, I am at odds with the world, I cannot change the world and I will not change myself. He goes down. We watch him go down and experience Aristotle's catharsis, which is the feeling of Yes, there was a time, somewhere back then, when I too felt at odds with the world, but I changed myself——I survived. I admire this man for going down, but I am nonetheless very glad I am not he. That's why tragedy makes you sad and relieved and respectful all at the same time. But the comic hero, he only half senses that he is at odds with the world. Thus he prosecutes his folly, and so steady is he that the wide world adjusts to him. That's why you laugh and feel gay and why you love a comic hero: he has maintained his madness and survived. Austin is neither, neither am I, for that matter. Austin is a failed evolutionary experiment, at least his condition is. Jose has his Genesis, and so do I. In the beginning there was matter, hydrogen atoms spread thinly through space. Except for one flaw they would have remained eternally content. But they were subject to gravitation (Original Sin). They were attracted to one another.

They fell together. Trillions of them, crashing toward a center. They were like workers pouring into the subway. The pressure at the center is enormous. Innocent atoms are squeezed mercilessly against one another. And what do they do? Disappear? O no, they combine into so-called higher forms of matter, more intricate elements, still more intricate molecules. At the periphery other hydrogen atoms arrive and add their center-striving weight. The tension becomes unbearable. Suddenly panic overcomes them and they explode, rush out. But the damage is done. The combinings have begun. Some combinations are ephemeral, others lasting. Everywhere molecules are making the fatal leap from the inorganic to the organic, and then from the static organic to the self-reproducing. Evolution is let loose in the universe, that agony of trial and error. Well, the rest is Darwin, but my point is that Austin is one of the countless futile experiments, one of the vain combinations. He may get back to the mainstream, and he may not. I really don't know which yet, but I couldn't dignify his situation as comic or tragic. You might say it's funny or sad, lucky or unlucky. But I know too much to deal in comedy or tragedy. Unfortunately. Anyway, Austin is depressed. He has met and had—and had and had—a beautiful woman. This was his heart's desire, but now instead of feeling pleasured he feels depleted. A ballful of his seeds has been planted in rich ground, but all of them are named Henry. Thus Austin decides to desert the Women's Building for the Men's Building. There the male patients are arranged according to the same scheme, on five floors in ascending nuttiness. Once again Austin chooses a room on the third floor. Higher the inmates would be too wild for his purposes, lower they would not be wild enough. In the center of the center floor he discovers an elegant fellow with live gray hair and a bright white mustache. The man, whose name Austin learns from the door card is Foxshuh, is sitting at a desk addressing an envelope with a straight pen. The tassels of his silk maroon robe dangle to the floor. Austin enters the room silently; nonetheless Mr. Foxshuh looks up. Yes, he says, can I help you? Mr. Foxshuh, Austin asks. That is how I am known here, he says, the appelation will suffice. My name is Austin. Yes, Mr. Foxshuh says. My name is Austin, Austin is impelled to repeat. Yes, Mr. Foxshuh says. Can you see me, Austin asks with sudden excitement, noticing how calm Mr. Foxshuh is. No, but why don't you sit down and tell me why you've come. You aren't frightened, Austin says suspiciously, why is that? Suppose you explain yourself, my dear fellow, after all I have not come into your quarters, you have come into mine with, I presume, a purpose. I've just come to talk with another human being, Austin says. Fine, proceed, Mr. Foxshuh says, giving Austin all his attention. Well, Austin says, takes a deep breath and begins to relate what has happened to him. Every now and then during the long recital an attendant or doctor passes the open door. At such instants Austin claps his hand over his mouth, and Mr. Foxshuh, not able to see Austin's apprehension but noticing the sudden silences, smiles and motions Austin to go on. You are perfectly safe here, he says, the administration is tolerant of voices on the third floor. Unless there is violence, we more or less have the run of our fantasies. So Austin goes on. Occasionally with an interrogatory intonation Austin inquires whether he is being understood, and Mr. Foxshuh nods assuringly, otherwise he is silent during Austin's story. So here I am, Austin concludes, do you believe me? The question has metaphysical connotations, Mr. Foxshuh says. It's a simple question, Austin protests. Is it? Well, instead of answering it suppose I explain to you what has happened to you, which would surely be more interesting than my judgment on your credibility. Mr. Foxshuh speaks so assuredly that Austin is filled with hope. You have defecated your floggis, Austin. My what? Your floggis, the floggis is the semisubstantial organ of opacity. Inorganic matter does not require a floggis in order to be seen, but the instant matter is imbued with life it develops a floggis. How do you know this, Austin asks. Mr. Foxshuh smiles bitterly. Would you believe me, Austin, if I told you that I once defecated my floggis, that once I was exactly in your situation? Why not, Austin says, unsure whether the man is a nut or not. My dear Austin, there are an estimated— estimated, that is, five years ago when I regained my floggis—three hundred thousand defloggites in America. Where are they all, Austin asks. They are, Mr. Foxshuh says, leaning forward and lowering his voice, everywhere. Everywhere, Austin exclaims. Everywhere, Mr. Foxshuh answers. Are there any in this room? Perhaps, Mr. Foxshuh says mysteriously. I mean, besides me. Perhaps, Mr. Foxshuh says again. You explained, Mr. Foxshuh goes on, that you were overwhelmed by a fear that you would be captured by scientists, subjected to experiments, perhaps vivisection. I didn't mention vivisection. Nonetheless, vivisection is a possibility, it would have occurred to you sooner or later. It occurs to all defloggites. All defloggites believe that if they fall into the hands of the opaques they will become laboratory animals, and even if the scientists left them alone the government could not afford to. Yes, yes, I feel that, Austin says. Exactly, your response is classic. Well, believing this, defloggites take great care not to be discovered. Some move to a warmer climate, where the elements will not cause them hardship. They live in woods and swamps. Some retreat to abandoned farmhouses or mountain cabins. Some live in untenanted summer houses during the winter and relinquished town houses in the summer. And some, like rats, lurk in the storerooms of restaurants and cafeterias, fearful of cold and hunger. But some— and Mr. Foxshuh pauses for effect. Yes, yes, Austin says excitedly. Some, the brightest and most enterprising, maintain contact with one another. These have formed a great organization. What is that, Austin asks breathlessly. The NAADP, Mr. Foxshuh announces in organ tones, the National Association for the Advancement of Defloggite People. Is there really such a group, Austin asks. Is this the kind of thing one could invent, Mr. Foxshuh says. No, Austin admits, but what does the organization do? Many things, primarily it reminds defloggites that they are not alone. Then—and very important —it maintains a constant search for flogges. For flogges,

Austin says. Yes, you see, man has reached such an intricate evolutionary stage that he can, unlike the lower organisms, separate from his floggis. The floggis, as you yourself experienced, is most often lost during defecation. Now, if the floggis is lost in a rural area serviced not by sewers but by cesspools it is relatively simple to reclaim. Expert floggis-finders visit the scene of the defloggation, open the cesspool, sift the contents, regain the floggis and return it to the owner. The owner ingests it and once more becomes opaque. What happens if the defloggite is a city dweller, Austin says. Then it's a much more complicated problem, as you can imagine. In fact, the prognosis for urban defloggites is not good. Nonetheless scavengers are always roaming the shores and beaches near the cities in the hope of discovering a floggis. Can a floggis be seen, Austin asks. No, but it can be felt. These dedicated beachcombers crawl through the light surf and over the hard sand at low tide, feeling with their hands. Occasionally—and more often than you might suspect—a floggis is found. In this case it is turned over to the ID committee. The ID committee, Austin says, what is that? The Identification Committee, a group of defloggites whose job it is to match the recovered floggis with its defloggite. Is that difficult? More than I can say, Mr. Foxshuh says, terribly time-consuming. The only known way to test whether a floggis belongs to a defloggite is for the defloggite to ingest it. If it belongs, the defloggite regains his opacity immediately. If it does not—and of course there are enormous odds against it belonging—the defloggite passes the alien floggis with his stools. But this takes anywhere from sixteen to twenty-four hours. Do they ever match one up, Austin says. Mr. Foxshuh smiles again. Look at me, he says. And you lost yours in the city? Yes, Mr. Foxshuh says, I was an urban defecator. I won't tell you how many flogges I had to ingest to find my own, it would prejudice you against trying it yourself, but the number was high. But what I don't understand, Austin says, is why you are here. Mr. Foxshuh hisses through his teeth, picks up a straight pen and breaks it in two like a pretzel. The NAADP, he says. I don't understand, Austin says. Well, Mr. Foxshuh says with a bitter sigh, defloggites who are restored to opacity—we call them refloggites— are sworn to secrecy. As you know from your own intense reactions to defloggation, a deep suspicion against the opaque world arises. Defloggites feel—perhaps with justice, perhaps not—that if their existence were to become known the opaques would hunt them down and either destroy or imprison them. As a result, before a refloggite is allowed to return to his normal life, he is told that should he reveal the existence of his former companions a terrible vengeance will be visited upon him. And you did this, Austin asked. No, no, of course not. I had sworn, and I am a man of honor. But, you see, I kept up my contacts with the NAADP, and it occurred to me that, if they would let me, I might make their existence known to a few trustworthy opaque scientists who could be of great help to them. You have no idea the handicaps we worked under, and here Mr. Foxshuh becomes quite excited. Suppose advanced methods of biological analysis were to be applied to the problems of matching floggis to defloggite, think of all the useless ingestions that could be by-passed. Do you know that I ingested over three thousand flogges—on occasion ten at a time—before I found my own. And do you know that every time I ate another defloggite's floggis I knew in my heart it wasn't mine. Then one day, while I was feeling around in a new batch, I had this overwhelming conviction that one of them would be mine. And it was. I gobbled them up, and suddenly I was my old self. The NAADP claims it was all my imagination, that it is quite common for a refloggite to feel, after the fact, that he had recognized his floggis before ingesting it. But I know what I know. So, I ask you, how can those poor fools, with their primitive methods of inquiry learn anything about defloggation? Also I suggested certain preventive measures, that floggis filters be fitted into all urban sewers, so that they never get out to sea. This could be accomplished only with the assistance of opaque authorities. Well, the NAADP listened to me and finally they seemed convinced. They not only would allow me to go ahead, but they would help me. What a laugh! They put me in touch with a certain petty official in Washington, saying they had reason to believe he could be trusted and would be sympathetic to my suggestions. Well, I now happen to know that this official is himself a refloggite, a dyed-in-the-wool refloggite. Ah well, don't let my bitterness embitter you. You are young, there is time for you. If you work hard, if you meet the right people, play the game, you may be able to return to the opaque world

—the outside opaque world, he added sadly. But how did you end up in here, Austin said, I still don't understand that. Mr. Foxshuh ground his teeth before answering, I went to see the man the NAADP directed me to, and while I was in his office telling my story he surreptitiously called a hospital to take me away. Then Mr. Foxshuh lapsed into silence, but Austin had become all keyed up. He wanted to know more. How can I contact this organization, he said, how can I begin the search for my floggis? Lethargically, as if he had lost all interest in the subject, Mr. Foxshuh explains that there is an alley off a certain street in the lower part of the city where a defloggite is on duty twenty-four hours a day. Merely enter the alley, call the word floggis, and you will be among them presently. Do they have a headquarters, Austin asks, a place to eat and rest and talk with other defloggites? Mr. Foxshuh passed a hand over his forehead. Young man, this has exhausted me, I am weary and must sleep. You no doubt would like to sleep yourself. Take my bed. I'm old, used to napping in chairs, I'll stay here, and Mr. Foxshuh shut his eyes. Austin was weary, he would have liked to crawl under the covers of Mr. Foxshuh's bed, but fear of an attendant or doctor passing and seeing the headless bump in the bedclothes led him to settle for the top of the bedclothes. Lying sideways, he pulled his legs near his chin for warmth and tucked his hands between his legs. In seconds he was asleep. How long he slept he did not know, but he was awakened by the shouts of Mr. Foxshuh, half directed to the hallway and half at him. Austin tried to move but

```
          BACK OF BEYOND BOOKS

      Tuesday November 10, 1992
           Cashier: WSS
        * - Non-taxable
----------------------------------------

QTY   ITEM                   LIST   PRICE
----------------------------------------

 1 NEW TITLE                 3.98    3.98
----------------------------------------

                  Sub-total:$   3.98
                       Tax:$   0.32
                     Total:$   4.30
              Amt tendered:$   5.00
                    Change:$   0.70

                      CASH:$   4.?

          HAPPY TRAILS!
```

was bound hand and foot in the fetal position by the cord of Mr. Foxshuh's robe. Hurry, Mr. Foxshuh shouted, I've caught one, I've caught one. Now you'll believe me. Hurry, and turning hatefully to Austin he said You little scab, you agent you, did you really think you fooled me? Doctor, doctor, hurry. Did you think you fooled me with your naive story, your patent lies? Doctor, nurse, come! They sent you, didn't they? They sent you to see if I was getting through to the fools here. What were you supposed to do if I was? Throttle me, throttle the old man who wanted to help them, who only wanted to help them? Well, now we'll see who comes out on top, you fink. Doctor, doctor! Frantically Austin pulled at the cord. Down the hall he hears running feet, and just as a doctor and a male nurse burst into the room, Austin snaps the cords and leaps from the bed. Get him, get him, Mr. Foxshuh yells. He's in here somewhere, close the door, close the door. Expertly the male nurse subdues Mr. Foxshuh and fixes him on the bed. The doctor stands by, syringe in hand, and with a single motion sticks it into Mr. Foxshuh's immobilized arm. Within seconds he is unconscious, and the male nurse covers him with the bedclothes. We haven't heard this sort of thing from him for a long time, the doctor says, prepare a room on the fourth floor. Yes sir, says the male nurse. Curtain falls.

✖ ✖ ✖ ✖ ✖ ✖ ✖ ✖ IS IT NO LETTERS because I said I was anti-semitic? If you want me to tell you I was kidding, I will. But I wasn't. I was shocked when Jose asked me whether I was a Jew. If suddenly a Jew who had thought I was a Jew asked me whether I was a Christian I wouldn't have been shocked perhaps, but I would have been displeased. I want to be both and more than either. Let me explain. Jews have been a big part of my life since I left high school. I could say that this was because they are warm and smart and receptive to other people's humannesses. That isn't the reason, however. I get along with Jews because their dreams and ends, as I understand them, are different from mine. A Jew wants to make it here and now, with people he can see and touch. I want to make it in the beyond and the past. The Jew is a thing of this world, he wins the bet, makes the deal, seduces the woman, discovers the particle, writes the poem. He is not concerned with perfection, but with achievement. The Jew is Aristotelian, I'm Platonic. Therefore the Jew is good for me. He never enters into folies a deux with me. Instead he brings me down and in, as I believe I bring him up and out, both ameliorating activities. Did I mean what I said then? Yes, the idea of the Jew has no aesthetic appeal for me, only a practical one. Whereas the idea of Jose, the anti-Jew, has great aesthetic appeal. He is all gesture, style and form. Jose is non-Euclidean geometry, infinitely various and useless. I explain this in the hope that you will not withdraw your friendship and your ear, because tonight I screwed away half my contacts with life. I had two dates, one with Mrs. Frank, a kind of, you should pardon the expression, standing date, and the other with Mary. Mary I had been putting off and putting off, so that I just had to see her, and I suggested a bar near where she lives for eleven-thirty. Eleven-thirty, she said. I told her I was still interviewing for MUI, and since she rates work over pleasure she agreed. When I told Mrs. Frank that I had to leave her at eleven she said Eleven! Yes, to see my mother, knowing that Mrs. Frank rates motherhood over pleasure. Thus I had the evening down to a workable timetable, sort of. In deference to my early departure Mrs. Frank prepared a six o'clock supper. Junior, as always, was all eyes, not eyes observant but eyes hungry, saying nothing spontaneously, just answering me with No sir and Mrs. Frank with No ma'am. Such a strange little boy, eunuchoid, white and soft and, I'm afraid, repulsive. You know that look some people have, if they touched you you'd turn into a blob? Like that. Well, Mommie did her best to hustle him off to sleepyby, but no sooner was he in than he got up to pee, drink water (which I knew would make more pee), come out to say good night. Also he called Mommie to close the window because there was a buzz outside, then open the window because he has hot and sweaty. And so on until ten o'clock, when it looked like he was out, and we hustled ourselves into the sandbox. After number one, Mrs. Frank in a playful mood asked me if I would ever consent to being circumcised. It seems that Jewish women develop less cancer of the poopoo than Gentile women, the apparent reason being that Jewish men are circumcised. I didn't at first see the connection, but when I did I told her that she had nothing to fear from me poopoo-wise because I washed behind my ears daily. But if I really wanted you to? I told her that, as I understood it, adult circumcision was somewhat more difficult than excising a hangnail. But if I really wanted you to? Let me think about it, I said, and got out of bed, ostensibly to think. Instead of thinking, however, I went to the bathroom and brought back a palmful of water. What's the water for? To cleanse you, I said. I wash behind my ears too, she said. How about behind your soul, I said, and threw a knee over her tummy. My soul, she said. Yes, I said, and poured the water on her forehead, saying the while I baptize you in the name of the Father, the Son, and the Holy Ghost. Did she bounce! Too late, I said, you're a shickse, at which point Junior walked in to report that the buzz was back. Funny about sex, when you're a kid you hide it from the adults, and when you're an adult you hide it from the kids. It seems that while I was getting the water I had unlocked the bedroom door. But see the picture, I'm sitting on Mommie's tummy, she's tossing and turning, trying to free herself. I jumped off, Mrs. Frank jumped into a wrapper, and I shut my eyes, I didn't want to look at anything, least of all myself in the bureau mirror. I don't know what explanation she gave the kid, but she was gone for half an hour, so that by the time she got back I was dressed. I thought she'd want me to stick around and talk and mend, but she was as glad to be rid of me as I was to go. I was forty-five minutes late for Mary, who was white, not with anger, just with waiting. She had paid for her one drink and was ready to leave. I apologized at length, inventing an account of an interview in which some really crucial points about the Experimental Sales Technique had been revealed. The minute, I said, the very minute I could, I hopped into a cab, I didn't even stop to call here. Where's your brief case, she asked. Jesus, and I looked around at my feet, I must have left it in the taxi. Why is your hair that way? I ran a hand over my hair. It was, as they say, in disarray. Was this one of those winning Freudian lapses that come up suddenly to crack you on the back of the skull? Probably, because I dropped the MUI bit and told her I had been fired, told her about Mrs. Frank, trying to make myself seem the victim of an older, worldly woman. I guess I wanted to let Mary have it in her Christianity. Well, she let me have it in the Oedipus. I could understand, she said, if you were in love with her, but just to go and take advantage of the woman like that, you obviously have no respect for her feelings, just as you have no respect for anyone's feelings, not even your mother's. Let's leave my mother out of this, I said half joking. I've seen your mother weep, she said, weep. What? I have, I've seen her weep at what you're doing to yourself. What am I doing to myself? Running with that bunch of degenerates. Degenerates, what degenerates? I didn't know what she meant, but I was soon to learn. To amuse her and, I guess, to shock her a little I had told her stories about the wilder urban types I had met. But these people aren't my friends, I said, they're just kinds you come across in any big city. You mean Harvey isn't your friend? Sure he is, or was, but is Harvey a degenerate because he sleeps with Mrs. Fox? You think that's all right, don't you? What's wrong, they both enjoy themselves, as far as I can see. Does that make it all right, that everyone enjoys himself? Yes, it does, I said, what's wrong with you, Mary, screwing is a practice millions of years old and common to many species. How about that Lesbian in your office? She was referring to the art director, who bunks with a bulldyke. I don't even know the woman, I said, she just happens to work there, what do you want me to do, go to confession and confess other people's sins? And this woman now, you can't tell me you didn't get that idea from Harvey. What idea, the idea you're talking about was implanted in me by Mother Nature, or from your point of view by God the Father. Idea, is there an idea in a male going to bed with a female, I said. Under the present circumstances, yes, there is. You came here right out of her bed with lies and stories, isn't there an idea in that? Why did you tell me about her, anyway? That was obviously a mistake, I said. I hope you don't think we're still engaged, she said, to which I was silent. Well, we're not, but I want to tell you something, it's all right for you to abuse me, I'll get over it, but please, please don't abuse your mother. What has my mother got to do with it? You didn't know, did you, that she goes to Mass every morning to pray for you. Thank you, Mother, for nothing. Mary, what do you want from me, I work hard, I make my bed in the morning, I take the garbage down at night, what do you want? I want you not to ruin your life, that's what I want. Your mother told me that her grandfather was like you and that he ruined his life and almost ruined the lives of his children. Mary, I don't know what you're talking about, do you understand me, I don't know what you're talking about. That's the tragedy of it, that you don't know what I'm talking about. You know what I ought to do, I said, I ought to go to that phone booth and call my mother and ask how much of this crap is hers and how much of it is yours. I wish you would, I wish you'd call her and ask what she really thinks about you, I've asked her to tell you, many times, but she says it wouldn't do any good, that it would only upset you. Mary, I think you're out of your mind, I think you're crazy. Do you think your mother's crazy too? If she said what you're saying I'd think she was crazy too. Then, I feel sorry for you. Mary, do you know what my mother wants me to do, she wants me to get a job in a so-called large organization, so I can work my way up to be vice president or something. That was months ago, Mary said, after your father died, when you didn't have a job, and do you think it would be demeaning to work for a large organization? Mary, I feel like I'm in a dream, you don't understand me, my father didn't understand me, my mother doesn't understand me, I'm a pricky bastard. I don't know what that means, she said. Apparently nobody understands anybody in this farce, I'm a pricky bastard, which means that I'm a difficult person, and to answer your question, yes, I do think to work for a big organization is demeaning. I'm a pricky bastard, just like degenerate Harvey and degenerate Jose, and I think everything is demeaning. I hate this city and I hate this country and I hate the stores and the movies and the buildings and the streets and the sky and the ground and the people and I hate you. You're right in there with the rest of it. Fuck you, Virgin Mary. Well, needless to say, she got up and left. For an instant I thought of following her to see that she got home safely, but then I decided that God's love and her own virtue would save her from night prowlers, and if they didn't she could be the first American saint to die protecting her chastity. As soon as she was gone, however, I remembered that Prudence had run away from me the same way. Both times I guess it was my fault, but I don't know how, do you know what I mean, I don't know how. Am I wrong in trying to be what I want to be and in doing what I do to become it? I never told you, but my mother did actually suggest that I go to work for a big organization, a department store or a textile house or something, and I was hurt or disappointed or whatever you want to call it, because if that's what they had in mind for me, my mother and father, why did they send me to school? Didn't they know that once you put a magic-seeker into the hands of teachers he's sunk? Books become the final goal, writers the final heroes.

You've seen us, all the poor slobs holed up in furnished rooms, working on fantastic projects that will solve their problems, spiritual and worldly. Think of us thousands and thousands of talentless shits whacking away, rewriting Tennessee Williams or J. D. Salinger or T. S. Eliot or, like me, Peter Pan. So I did call up my old lady. It was after midnight, and she wanted to know if I was in jail, had been drinking, in a fight, rapped up the Austin, killed somebody. No-no, no-no, but they acted like double negatives, the more I denied the more she imagined. If I wanted her to come and get me she would, if I was in trouble and needed money she'd bring it, if I was sick she'd get a doctor. Well, after she had exhausted all the catastrophes and I all the denials, we were left with the reason I had phoned. All right, I said, I want to know what you think of me. She understood. You're my son, she said. That's not the information I asked for. I love you very much, she said. You mean you love me like a son, but I want to know what you think of me, not as your son, but as somebody else's son. How can I think of you except as my own son, she said. Make the effort. I think you're a very fine person, she said. All right, I'm a very fine person, but do you think I'll make out, will I make out in this life? Will I get what I want, no, what I need? I think you will, she said. What's the qualification in your voice, come on, tell me. You think I'll make out, if. If what? Tell me! Why don't you come up here, you can sleep on the couch, and we'll talk about it tomorrow morning. I want to talk now, I'm not going to sleep on the couch or anywhere until I find out what the if is.

No answer. Mom? Finally she said she didn't know what the if was. But there is one, isn't there? There's an if for everyone, she said. No, there isn't, and you know there isn't, some people have it made from the start. I'm not one of those, am I, am I? No, she said. Jesus, I could hear her crying and I wanted to withdraw the questions, withdraw the call, I had awakened her and made her hysterical. Mom, I think I know what the answer is, I've got it now. But she had become incoherent. My uncle was in the background, and finally he got on, full of querulous stupidity. His judgments I didn't need and hung up. So here I am, home, writing to an estranged correspondent. Well, I do have the answer. When I pull this sheet of paper out of the typewriter I'll put another one in, and then another, and then another, and I won't leave this room until I finish the book. That's my answer.

ϗ ϗ ϗ ϗ ϗ ϗ ϗ IF YOU'RE READING this letter first, stop and read the other one. I could have asked my mother to mail it six days ago, but I didn't want to take the chance that she might open it. She's not a snooper, but she's worried and she might have thought she could help me with the information. I'll explain. And another thing. I may have to break this off and send you what there is, which you won't understand, but then I'll write again as soon as I can. I'm sitting on the bed, type-writer on lap, sweatlets dripping down my arms inside the pajamas. I almost feel like having a cigarette, which is something. I won't, though. Anyway, after I finished the other letter, which, by the way, I'm glad I still have, just as a record of that night, I began on Austin. I said to myself that I wouldn't eat or sleep or go to the bathroom, I'd just write and write until I was done or until I dropped dead. Don't ever threaten yourself like that, someone inside might be listening and take it seriously. Well, I brought Austin out of the nuthouse. Dawn was up by this time, not for Austin, for me. His parents' summer place occurred to him. They were in the city, and an emergency key was taped under the back-porch railing, as, by the way, it really was when I was a kid. So by side-stepping passengers on the train and by hoofing the final two miles, he gets to the bungalow. At last he feels safe. The house reminds him of his childhood vacations. His plan is to stick a while, eat and sleep, generally pull himself together, determine a plan for the future. Per-haps he'll go back to the city in a week or two and try to contact the NAADP. Why not? His situation is no more incredible than the existence of defloggites comb-ing beaches, poking around in cesspools. If there really is an NAADP he wonders if he will recognize any of his fellow members. Maybe that's what happened to Judge Crater. He's sorry he didn't ask Mr. Foxshuh whether a theory of defloggation had ever been developed, whether there wasn't something unique in the background of de-floggites to account for their condition. Well, he'd find out soon enough. Right now he's hungry, and he discovers some canned goods, asparagus tips, a Polish ham, pear halves in heavy syrup. Also a quart of green paint for the house trim. I'm sorry my parents sold the place before I knew you. You'd have liked it. I had a great ball there, the place gave me two distinct sets of friends, summer friends and winter friends. My best summer friend became a Jesuit—quite a different fish from Francis—a thoughtful guy who really wanted to spread the word. I never answered his letters because all that occurred to me to write about was my anti-Catholicism, and I didn't feel that was in the best of taste. I mean, the guy was slugging his way through the terribly severe initial Jesuit training. Maybe I should have let him reconvert me. What a boost for a seminarian! Anyway, Austin eats and thinks, no plan forms, he gets lonelier and lonelier, lonely to the point of desperation. Suddenly an idea comes. Who needs the NAADP to get opaque again? He'll use the green paint. So he pries open the can and with an old stiff brush does himself in front of the mirror, laying it on thick and even, just as he had so many times to the house under his father's direction. At first it's a miracle, he has the same sense of accomplishment a person feels the one and only time he tries an oil painting. But as he progresses he is overcome with horror. His open eyes are empty sockets, his mouth a hole through which he can see into the paper-thin hollow of his head. Little spots that he had missed on his scalp admit points of light, which shine on the inside of the paint. He is like the self he sometimes sees in nightmares, mottled and disgusting, frightening, outrageous. So he takes a bottle of turpentine and for three hours works to remove the paint. At the end, when the turpentine is gone and the bathroom floor is covered with soiled towels, clumps of toilet paper and a bedsheet torn into hand-size squares, he looks like a pale green ghost. His hair is matted and stringy. Now he is a genuine prisoner. He had considered gay afternoon raids on the local food and liquor stores, dips into the sea, sunbaths on deserted stretches of beach, but now he will be able to go out only on moonless nights, like some loathsome rodent. Then this shitty thing happened to me. I didn't know what else to write. I mean, I realize some parts of the book are maybe pretty good and others stink, but I was never in the situation before of not being able to write anything. I had him standing in front of the mirror feeling completely hopeless. He really didn't know what to do, and I didn't know what to do for him. But I was afraid to stop, I had promised myself I would finish the book before I got up from the desk or something bad would happen to me. All right, I said, I'll just type random words until this passes, maybe even they'll indicate Austin's confusion and I'll be able to leave them in. But no words came. All right, I'll keep the typewriter going by hitting unrelated keys, but I couldn't even do that. And then suddenly there was an emptiness in my chest. My heart stopped. Wait a minute, that scares me. I'm going to walk around the room a little. I'll be right back. OK, I thought it was going to happen again, but I'm OK. Christ, ever since that night, except when I'm asleep, I feel it's going to happen again. It's like being dipped in liquid fear, and there's nothing I can do. If running would help I'd run, if screaming I'd scream. There's one thing that works sometimes. I pray. I say Jesus, please don't let me die, and it helps sometimes. Sometimes it gets worse. It's only happened once, you know, my heart actually stopping, and then just for about five seconds, but it's the fear that it will happen again that gets me. If it happens again I think I will die. I mean, how many times can your heart stop without dying? Like right now the fear is hovering. I'm not in it, I'm still writing, but it's there. This is the first time I've touched the typewriter since the night, and I guess that accounts for it. Well, I'll just keep writing. But if I stop, you'll know. It doesn't mean that I've died or anything, only that I've become afraid. Anyway, somehow I got to Jose's room, it was locked, but I knocked and knocked until he opened. Don't get excited, I said, but I think I've had a heart attack. Do you know that crazy nun was in his room, I didn't see her, she was in the bathroom, but later that night, after the doctor came and gave me a shot, and I was waiting to pass out, he told me. She actually walked out of the school and is shacking up with him. I shouldn't say shacking up, because I suspect he sleeps on the floor, but she's in there. Jose has promised to bring her in here to meet me, but my mother has been around almost all the time. Well, good old Jose hustled me back to my room, plunked me on the bed and over my protestations brought back from next door a myopic, bull-necked doctor named Ernest Curtin. Half asleep he was, thick in the mouth, but nervous withal. Jose had told him The Heart, and, true, it beat wildly in my throat. Beat, I thought, beat however you want, but beat. When I heard the doctor's name it sunk me down. Curtains, I thought. Meanings gathered. I considered the date so that I could be aware, before the fact, of when I died. He died on this day, one, two, five years ago. We go to the cemetery each anniversary, even when it rains. No flowers, just a visit, for sentiment's sweet sake. There is a young tree twenty paces from his grave, we can see its growth each twelve-month's time, it will outlast us all, but most it will outlast this nice young man whose every organ flowed with juice but one. Jesus, I said, I don't want some smell-breathing priest blowing up my nose, I want you, Jesus, the only one who ever made sense to me, I said in my head, lying on top of the bedclothes, shivering though the early morning was warm, and answered Curtin's questions. Any pain, tingling in the arms, numbness in the extremities, shortness of breath, nausea, dizziness? All the symptoms of my father's heart attack. No, no, everything was no. The only thing that happened to me was my heart stopped, I told him, but he didn't seem interested in that. Finally I squeezed up my courage and said Did I have a heart attack? We can't tell till we take an EKG, he said. An EKG, is that like a BM? We may have to take a BM too, he said. I took a BM before supper last night. Basal metabolism, he said, and after wrapping up his blood-pressurer he took out his needle. No, I said. This will put you to sleep for a few hours. No. You'll be hungry afterward. No needle, I said. I insist, he said. No. It will relax you, he said. I'm not leaving this scene. Do you want to have a real heart attack, he said, which convinced me. Shoot, I said, and he shot. Don't move for a week, he said, don't get out of bed, then we'll take an EKG and see. It sounded like a commercial. You'll feel drowsy in a few minutes. I doubt it. You will. OK, I said, certain that I wouldn't. Then he wrapped up his needle and talked low to Jose before leaving. I expected Jose to come back with the poop. Did I have a heart attack or not, I said. Jose shrugged. How do you feel? Scared. Pain in the chest, tingling in the arms? And he asked me all the doctor's questions over again. It was a circus, he knew even less than I. What did he say out there, I said. That you shouldn't get out of bed, that you'd be asleep in a few minutes, that you'd wake up hungry, that someone should stay with you, do you feel drowsy? No. Don't tell my mother, Jose, promise me, I don't want to worry her, and he promised and then told me about Cousin Rita-Sister Barbara. According to Jose the nuns had not detained her. The day of the morning she promised to come to Jose's room she had begun menstruating and gone to bed. She menstruates with anguish, he said, I remember it well from the time I lived with her family. Like labor pains, four days. When we have children she will be prepared, he added. So I wasn't wrong the night we had the fight, I said. Fight, fight, that was not a fight, when a Spaniard fights someone dies. No symptoms, I said, and I guess I was feeling better. I knew that Jose, despite his promise, would tell my mother, and I was glad. I hadn't been upset at the idea of causing my mother distress, that's what mothers are for. I was upset because she might jinx me. She had vigiled my father away and now she might vigil me away. But, no, her wisdom in treating childhood diseases would overcome the jinx. She would save me. And if she didn't, Jesus would. I couldn't miss. I must have been weary to the hair. In fact I remember, the night of the heart, writing about Austin, how flat and lifeless my hair felt. Well, when I woke up, late in the afternoon, my mother was there and I was hungry. I ate two bowls of oatmeal, an orange, lots of toast, and drank a quart of milk. I would eat only good foods, the foods my mother had given me as a boy. I would build up my bones and muscles, and as soon as I was able I would get out and soak up the sun. I would get lots of sleep, not strain my eyes, not say bad words or think bad thoughts. And particularly I would never write again. Somehow that had been the unbearable stress. Who had to write? For what? I would cultivate my body. I would grow in strength and purity, I would grow up to be a civil engineer, make bridges, which all people, mostly I, understand. I want to lie down now. I'm frightened again.

❈ ❈ ❈ ❈ ❈ ❈ ❈ ❈ THIS MORNING I was dying, this afternoon I'm living. I'm soaked with sweat, I'm smoking a cigarette, I intend to smoke many cigarettes, I intend to play tennis in the heat, go to the beach, swim out until my arms ache and trust to second wind to get back. When I see the Lady Frank again I intend to break my own magnificent record. But this morning I was crossing the street, a car zipped around the corner, and I held up my hand like an old man. I could have jumped out of the way, but do you see the logic, if I jumped I would die from a heart attack, whereas if I stopped, the car might stop. It stopped, the driver frowned through the windshield, but then he merely looked. So young, he thought, what is it, cancer of the crotch, busted pedal balls? I had held up my hand like an old man, and I'm twenty-one. Eight days ago I was tearing beer cans in two, pieces off ladies like leaves from a pad. O but now I must not tinker with the ticker, must watch veins for pains. Except for the few hours yesterday, when I wrote to you, all last week I lay in bed immobile, waiting for the emptiness. Every tickle, every gurgle, and I made ready to die. If the tip of my thumb became numb, it was a small embolism cutting off the blood to the part of my brain that controlled the tip of my thumb. I could feel it in my head. At other times I decided I had leukemia, that my heart had stopped because of a diminishment of red blood cells below the beating threshold. I asked my mother to bring me a hand mirror, with which I secretly examined my gums. Yes, they were telltale gray. I asked for a needle and after sterilizing it over a lit match drew a drop of blood from my now unnumb thumb. It seemed pink rather than red. Good, I preferred leukemia, at least I would die slowly, and what time was left would not be spent in suspense. When Curtin came on the leukemia day I told him my diagnosis. He said he doubted that I was right but, if I wished, a blood test could be taken in his office when I visited him. Which was today. All through the week he was so definite about when I could get up that I was sure he knew exactly what was wrong with me. If I pressed him, however, he backed away. The EKG will tell us a lot, he said, it won't tell us everything, but it will tell us a lot. Like what, I asked. We'll have to see. If I pass, does that mean I'm OK? Not necessarily, he said. You mean, if I am OK, really, I'll never be sure of it again? This made him philosophical. Life is a process of dying, he said, and the EKG is a limited diagnostic tool. He was the limited diagnostic tool. Every day he came he filled me with new vacuums of uncertainty. Nor were my other visitors much better. They had that distant look of tragedy beneath their smiles and reassurances. O everybody came, I felt like Dean Swift observing his mourners. Even Wally from MUI. The mutt. Give me a guy with a little heart trouble, he said, they last forever. You know why, he added, they take care of themselves. My brother was fifty-three when he had his heart attack and he lived to sixty-four. That gives me eleven years, I thought, I'll be thirty-two, won't even beat Christ. And you know why, Wally repeated, he took care of himself. Give him somebody with a little heart trouble, that's what Wally says. He also brought Fox's best, without, by the way, an offer of the job back. Which who wants? But I thanked Wally, it was nice of him to have come, and I told him to thank Fox, while saying in my heart—no, my liver—fuck you, Harry Fox, and your crummy spy work. The most frightening was Harvey, because he was frightened. He couldn't even summon up the smile, he wasn't hypocrite enough, he just stood there at the foot of the bed nodding and flapping his hands against his sides, about to say something and saying nothing. When he left I was doomed. I was sure he had heard something from Jose or Curtains or my mother, something lethal. How many hundreds of times, lying there, did I panic, waiting for the thing, the final gasp? A hundred hundred, that's how many. Best, I guess, was Mary. She took over from my mother when my mother had to go and do, and she was steady-on. Whether it was her Catholic stoicism or a simple confidence that nothing was wrong with me, I don't know, but she was her exact usual self. They have the same quality, Mary and my mother, I almost could die in the presence of one or the other without bitterness. And in his fashion Jose was good too. He suggested that I rise and dress and we visit a Puerto Rican cat house of his acquaintance, where, he claimed, one purchase would set all my innards right. And he kept offering me Cognac, but I had no taste. I wanted clarity, an open and empty head. With such, at times, I argued myself out of the conspiracy of death that surrounded me. I would be well again, and the important thing thereafter would be to breathe, walk, look, be. No writing, never writing again. Other times I wished Prudence was here, and still others when I was glad she wasn't. She was, after all, one of the unresolved dilemmas that had gathered on me like successive weights. Once or twice I thought of slipping out to see Lady Frank, but memory of the boy kept me still. I read the complete novels of Jane Austen—I think because she has a name like my hero's and yet is so different from him—but I can't remember now a single character or situation. It was like reading comic books, but for the time that I read she saved me from questioning the integrity of my cardiovascular system, and for that I will always think of her fondly. Well, this morning was my moment of truth. Cardioquack let me get up to come down to his office. He put me on his leather table, took my pulse and remarked with surprise that I wasn't nervous, which made me nervous. Should I be nervous, I said. No, no, the calmer you are, the more we'll be able to tell, and he plugged in his electrocardiograph, eagerly adjusted wires and disks to my chest. Soon the telling paper rolled out like quiet tickertape. The needle swung as he moved the disks to different portions of my flesh. Big healthy sweeps the needle took, it seemed to me. But he frowned. Ooops. Finally he was done, tore off the tape and took it to his desk, frowning, frowning. Be patient, he said, this will take a little time, and to reckon he picked up a two-foot ballpoint pen, from which dangled a chain of tiny tin spheres. I didn't understand why the pen was so long. A special tool doctors use to decipher electrocardiograms? Then I realized it was a gag pen. This clown was deciding my fate with a Coney Island gag pen. After forever he put it down with a sigh of accomplishment. No damage, he said. Did you think there would be damage, I said, which he ignored. However, he said, there's strain. What? Strain. What do you mean? There's a certain strain on the heart. I don't understand, I said, my breath came quick and shallow. Your heart is under a strain. We both pondered this for a while. Finally he said Are both your parents alive? My father's dead. Hmm, he said, what did he die from? A heart attack. His face made a quick little dance. Doesn't mean a thing, he said. How old was he? Seventy-one. You see, doesn't mean a thing. I didn't say it meant anything, I said. Exactly, he said. I waited, but he seemed to slip into a contemplation. We sat there, I on the leather table, he on a swivel chair turned out from his desk toward me. Panic rose. What should I do, doctor? Suddenly he was professional self-containment. Just take it easy, he said, as if addressing an idiot child, in a month the cardiogram will be clean. You could go out and get a million dollars' worth of insurance from any company in the world. Do I need insurance, I said. No, no, but you could if you wanted to, you're not married, are you? No, I said. Then why would you want insurance? You're mother is provided for, isn't she? Are you telling me something, doctor? No, no, I just want you to take it easy, you may never have another of these attacks as long as you live. How long will I live? Why, you're a young man, he said. I know, but how long will I live? He laughed a great big—you should pardon the expression—hearty laugh. You're practically a boy, you shouldn't be thinking of death. I'm trying not to, I said. Well, then don't, he said and got up from his swivel chair in a fatherly manner, then don't. Look, may I ask you some questions? That's what I'm here for, he said. Exactly what can I do and not do? You can do anything, in moderation. What do you mean, in moderation? I mean, don't overdo, which goes not only for you but for me and for everyone. What's don't overdo, don't overdo what? Don't get excited, for one thing, why are you getting excited? How can I not get excited if I'm excited? Obviously you're very excitable, he said. I certainly am, may I ask you another question? He waved his hand generously. Is there a possibility this whole thing is emotional, I was pretty upset the night this happened, you know. There may be a certain psychic component in the physical condition, he said. But there definitely is a physical condition, is that it? Well, let me show you, he said, and he brought over the tickertape. You see these peaks, they should go up to here. That's twice as high as they actually go, I said. Exactly, now each day they'll go a little higher, and in a month they'll be up to here, he pointed to the desired level. So there's nothing to worry about, just take things easy. I was silenced. What are you

worried about, tell me and we'll clear it up. You can have
sex, if that's what's on your mind. I wasn't thinking about
sex, I said, in fact that was about the farthest thing from
my mind. Then what? I want to know if I can jump up
and down. Here? Yes. Do you want to? No, but I want
to know if I can. If you don't want to, why worry about
it? Because I do, it's like getting excited, I can't help it,
now will you please tell me if I can jump up and down
here and now. Do you mean are you physically able to,
he said. I do not mean that, and you know I do not mean
that, I mean would I drop dead if I did. It's unlikely. But
it could happen, is that it? It could happen to me, he said.
That's not my question, my question is could it happen
to me? It could happen to any of us. Well, we went on
like this for Christ knows how long, and it turned out
that I couldn't—or shouldn't—run, smoke, drink,
worry, stay up late, jump up and down, and it would be
better if I had intercourse lying on my back. It was after
leaving his office this morning that, like an old man, I
stopped the car on the street. I didn't know what to do
or where to go, so I walked. No, I shuffled. I shuffled for
miles. There was no one I wanted to see. What would I
have said? I have heart strain, I came here to tell you
this, how about spot of sherry and a turn in the garden.
Anyone for intercourse, me on my back? So I walked
and walked, and suddenly I found myself in front of Dr.
Newman's office near the college. The instant I saw his
plaque I knew I had been heading there all the time. His
receptionist said that ordinarily the doctor sees patients
only on appointment, but I must have looked a mess, be-

cause she said she would see if he could make an exception for me. Well, the guy listened for two goddamned hours. I told him, I guess, my whole life, about Mary and Prudence and my mother, about Fox and Professor Duffy, about high school and college, I even told him the plot of my novel. And after it was done he took me into his examination room, I got undressed, and he gave me the works, from top to toe, including another electrocardiogram. Boy, there was no ballpoint pen with this guy, he read it right off the machine. There's nothing organically wrong with you, he said when all the evidence was in. Why did Dr. Curtin say there was? I don't know, he said. Why did this thing happen to me, why did my heart stop? Your heart didn't stop, if your heart had stopped you would have died. Then what happened to me? I don't know, he said, but there was such discretion in his statement of ignorance that I was filled with confidence. It seemed to me, almost, that, if he didn't know, it wasn't worth knowing. May I ask you a question, I said. Yes. Can I jump up and down here in your office? Yes, he said. I might really do it. Go ahead. Can I smoke? Yes. Can I drink? Yes. Stay up late? Yes. Can I worry, I said, which made him smile. Can I have intercourse, me on top? Yes, he said, and suddenly his professional restraint disappeared, what did that doctor tell you about intercourse? He said I should lie on the bottom. Dr. Newman made a noise of pained disgust. Can I have intercourse five times a night? You're not trying to make me envious, are you, he said. Can I run around the block when I leave here? I guess I was pushing him because he repeated that there was nothing organically wrong with me, that in fact people with my build live longer than average. This sounded like horseshit, which he must have seen, because he wrote down the name and date of the medical journal that contained a study on longevity and physical types. I was satisfied, almost. When I leave here, I said, I'm going down to the river and run one mile, and the sun is out, is that OK? Come back and see me in a month, he said. You didn't answer my question. I'd prefer that you go home and write your novel. But I can run a mile if I want to, because I'm going to, you know. All right, he said, and after I got dressed he said it isn't easy to bare one's mind and one's body in the same day. It depends on who's looking, I said, and he understood the compliment. As he took me to the door of his office he said that he had liked my father and that I reminded him of my father. He wasn't a coward like me, though, was he? Your father knew he was going to die, Dr. Newman said and told me he had seen hundreds of people die and that either months or seconds before it happened a veil passed over them that relieved them of fear, and as I walked across the waiting room, which was filled with people who had had appointments for my two hours, he called out Finish your book. Everybody looked up at me, a Writer. If you don't want me to send you letters you'll have to write and say so. Otherwise they do me too much good to stop.

❋ ❋ ❋ ❋ ❋ ❋ I ARRIVED YESTERDAY. I always thought Italy was full of wops. In fact I had counted on being disappointed, the way I was when my mother first took me to Washington. But, Jesus, I walk by a pasteria where the windowed drawers have spaghetti in fifty shapes and sizes, pass a pretty girl, smile, she smiles back, watch a policeman in white direct traffic like an orchestra conductor, turn a corner and find the Colosseum lit by gold-blue light. I buy a large firm peach, and look. You've been here. Why didn't you tell me I was wasting my life in America? I'm never going home, I'll just sit down on the curb and die here. I flew Al Italia. I figured if I was going to a strange land without the language I might as well begin at the beginning, and as I walked up the ramp I knew something important in my life was happening. Ever since I was a child there was a secret rubber band from me to, something, my bed, my mother, something. The rubber band would not take too much stretching. I always wanted to get back to It, whatever It was. But the day before yesterday, when I boarded the plane, there was no rubber band. I think I may have left it in Dr. Newman's office. The stewardess looked like Monica Vitti, blond, a broad open face like a white horse, and she smiled at me. She smiled at everyone, I guess, but that didn't matter, the smiling had begun. What can I say, ever since I left I've been coming from all my body's seven apertures. I got a seat next to a tight-lipped business type, who held his brief case to his belly all the way to Europe. Later I found out he was Swiss. But across the aisle was the goods, a tremendous wop, half child half grownup, thirty-nine although he looked twenty-five, hairy, baby-faced, immense. His name was Mario. Fasten Seatbelts, Monica Vitti came down the aisle offering hard candy from a basket. Prego, she said, prego, and I thought I knew my first Italian word. Prego: candy. Well, Mario grabbed her. At first I thought it was an uninhibited male gesture. No, he was scared. She took his hand, spoke soothing Italian phrases. He listened, nodded, finally accepted the candy and sucked away on it for dear life. Off the ground, Unfasten Seatbelts, and he eased some. But then we landed at Boston to fill up the passenger list, and he wanted to get off. The stewardess patted him on the cheek. I think she would have given him mother's milk if he had asked and she had had. Can you see Miss Pan Am doing that? Well, as I watched them I was sort of sorry I wasn't scared myself, but I've never been so unfrightened. There actually was danger, I guess, not much, but some, and it relieved me completely of the illusory danger I'd been suffering since the night of the heart. Anyway, I got into the act, told Mario that thousands of planes were flying over different parts of the earth at that very moment, and the chances of anything happening to one of them were insignificant. Well, my American logic and

Monica's sympathetic Italian kept him aboard. After we rose out of Boston I offered him my pint of Scotch. At first he was afraid he'd chuck it up, but swallow led to swallow, and before long he was rosy and loose, telling me the story of his life. During World War II he had deserted the Italian army and through artful country-hopping gotten to relatives in the States. This was his first trip home, and he was afraid there might still be some avenging Black Shirts around. Haven't you seen any Italian movies, I said, the Italians have disowned the war, and the poor slob told me that after the war he had gone to an Italian movie but it made him so nervous he had to leave and hasn't been to another one since. Also he thought that his father, whose letters he never answered, would be angry with him. I told him that any father should be overjoyed to see his son again after so much time, and if he wasn't, fuck him. Fuck him, Mario repeated. He told me that I looked Italian, which, combined with Jose's occasional claim that I look Spanish, Mrs. Frank's that I look Jewish, and Mary's that I'm pure Irish whatever my blood and appearance, sort of makes me the universal man. I adore being adopted like this, I guess because in my heart I don't feel American and would like to be something. Objectively it was a compliment, too, Mario saying that I looked Italian, which I appreciate now after seeing the grace and dignity of Romans. At one point Mario leaned over the aisle to assure me that I wouldn't have any trouble finding girls in Italy, and when I said I planned to meet someone there he touched my arm and said I'd be OK then. Was

POWDERED EGGS   185

this what Italy would be like, I wondered, everybody understanding everything? And it is. The people look at each other in the street. It's fantastic, it's human. Two days here, and America seems like a long B-movie. Mario asked me if he could share the Scotch with his seatmate, a Parmesian chick, who after two years in the States was going back to Italy to get married. Of course he could. I didn't need Scotch when, over the business-man's brief case, I could see the moonlit clouds like cot-ton dipped in silver. It was the middle of the night but the stewardess had to draw the window curtains to let the passengers sleep. I tried to sleep, but I couldn't, Mario was attempting the impossible with his seatmate. It must have come to something because finally he slumped back and dozed off. A little later, the Parmesian chick leaned forward to peek at me—I was the only one who might have seen them wrestling—but I kept my eyes half closed, which reassured her. Then still later, when she had dozed off and Mario was awake, he whispered to me that he thought she was not a happy girl. She didn't really want to marry the boyfriend in Parma, she liked Americans. That was so sad to hear in that plane over the ocean at night. Why don't you marry her, I said to Mario. He frowned, he was married already, had four kids. Why don't you, he said to me. I will, I said. Good, he said, which seemed to settle something, and we both dozed off. Well, we stopped for twenty minutes at the Paris airport. I got out to stretch myself, stood on tippy-toe to see at least the Eiffel Tower. We were too far away, but at least never again will I have to say I've not been to Paris. Then on our way to Milan, Mario and the girl began tightening up. Also a number of the other passengers had lost their smiles. They couldn't all be returning prodigals, and now that I've seen Rome I don't understand. Is it that Italy is the one country in the world kinder to guests than natives? Well, Mario and I parted at Ciampino Airport in Rome. We promised to get together in the States, but we never will. In America he's a big wop who runs a gas station and I'm a city boy with artistic intentions, and this was very sad. Here I think we could be buddies, but America casts a cold light and a colder eye. I'm down already. O I'm still here, the slits of light in the tall shutters closed against the late west sun, the large bed under the clay-covered spread, the high ceiling of carved moldings, the exquisite but sturdy desk, all tell me that I'm still here, but I'm sad because sooner or later I'll have to go back. Ah well, sempre avanti. I arrived at this hotel and presented my passport to the porter. He looked it over. Yes, he had my reservation, he said in English, but would I wait a moment, Signor Martello the owner wants to see me, and after a word of French to another guest, a word of German to still another, alternating with comments in Italian to his assistant, he phoned Signor Martello to say that I, I had arrived. Signor Martello appeared immediately, took my hand in both of his, expressed deep gratification at my presence. I was tired from the trip, he understood, but would I do him the kindness of joining him for a drink? He apologized for his English, which was limited but elegant, apologized for his hotel, which was unlimited and elegant. I protested. No, no, he owned five hotels in Rome, and this was the least. He would show me his hotel on the Via Veneto. Christ, I thought, whom had he mistaken me for? He'd be furious when he found out I was only me. Then it came out. You are a literary man, he said as the drinks arrived. Ah, the passport. Under Occupation I had written Writer. The porter was apparently with orders to direct all Writers to Signor Martello. You write for the press, he asked. No, I'm a novelist. Ah, he shivered with pleasure. His son-in-law was also a novelist, I must join his family for dinner tonight, his son-in-law and I will have much to discuss. So we had another drink, and he told me that when I got to my room I should give whatever of my clothes had been wrinkled in transit to the maid and they would be ready for me after my nap. Ceremoniously he turned me over to the porter, who with frightening deference turned me over to the bellboy, who with even greater deference escorted me to this large silent room, whereupon I flopped in yonder bed without so much as visiting the marble bathroom. At dinner there was something of a language barrier. Signor Martello was the only one with English. Everything his wife, daughter, son-in-law said had to filter through him. But the food was great. What's with Italian cooking in America? That's not Italian food, it's a base for condiments. The evening was mild. The attention of the waiters, and the knowledge that lovely Rome lay about me like a sweet cunt filled me with good will. It would have been perfect except for the son-in-law. This was the novelist, who turned out to be just a hack writer of magazine serials. It was divine justice. I had been described to him as a novelist, and when he learned that I had not actually published anything he wouldn't talk to me. He'd talk, even say things for my benefit, but he wouldn't address me directly. Signor Martello did his best to translate. At one point the son-in-law must have expressed some particularly dirty sentiment about America, because Signor Martello swallowed, burbled and failed to follow with the English. Seeing this, the son-in-law spoke directly to me in French. I knew it was French, but otherwise, Jesus! He repeated himself in German. Then in Spanish, as if speaking to a delinquent child. Finally back into French, which I did understand, he said to the table at large Il parle un langage seulement? Boy, I could have smacked him with a wet spaghetti. How to explain about Americans, that they can study languages for years in school and still not be able to buy a pot in the market place. Well, I looked at him steady-on and emitted a long series of nonsense syllables filled with chs and zhs. Everyone was puzzled. I explained to Signor Martello that I had addressed his son-in-law in Russian. But I do not know Russian, the son-in-law said. Not know Russian, I said, next to English it is the most important language in the world. No reply. I considered doing the same in Chinese, but decided not to push my luck. Well, I was vindicated, even though I'm still afraid of being asked down to the desk to interpret for some monolingual Russian guest. I don't know when I'm going to get to see Prudence. I chose Signor Martello's hotel, you know, because that's where Prudence's letter came from, but by the time I got here she had left for Venice. The porter called her Venice hotel for me, but she had left Venice too, and there was no forwarding address because she planned to come back, although the hotel didn't know exactly when. If you want to write, write here. If I've left, they'll forward.

✻ ✻ ✻ ✻ ✻ ✻ ✻ I'M NOT THROWING coins in the fountain, but I have fixed it to get back to Rome. This morning I went to St. Peter's, which disappointed me. No patina, all was shining brightly. There was even a guy on a scaffold polishing the goldware. O it was big, an indoor Grand Canyon, but what I like most about Rome is the attitude of Romans toward it. There's so much history around they can forget history. I don't mean forget it, I mean Rome's past is accounted for, nothing has to be done with it. It's accomplished. The least of these brown and rosy people seems to know he's more important than the largest of the dead. And I wonder if we know that in America. I mean, no one ever asked me, but suppose someone had, someone said How do you rate yourself beside George Washington? Well, I'd wrinkle up and claim it was a silly question. But it's not a silly question, and I have an

answer: I am to George Washington as infinity to noth-
ingness. I'm alive, he's dead, and even if I was only
barely alive and he was only just dead, the proportion
would be the same. America's past is recent and scattered,
we haven't solved it or settled for it. As a result, someone—maybe a teacher, a parent, a writer—someone who
has wangled his way into my esteem lets me know that
George Washington is more interesting to him than I
am. This is not as it should be. I can sneeze on this someone, whereas George Washington has to squeeze through
a crack of gone time with words and relics. When I
sneeze I am no construction from faded evidence. Well,
all right, you say, but what has this guy's possibly
faulted values got to do with me? He has impressed me,
this teacher-parent-writer, he is an impressive guy,
America has put him up and forth, and I absorb his attitude about me, I come to feel that way about myself.
Look, even while you're reading this, you're saying I've
got some hubris putting George Washington down in my
own favor. But why shouldn't I if it helps me to be? I
bet there isn't a wop in Rome who feels he is less than
Constantine. It's the wop who's got the gism, uses sun
and air. Constantine is only an idea in the wop's head,
an arrangement of electric stresses in his head, and if
they should relax, ever so slightly, there would be no
Constantine. Well, according to me, Romans understand
this, so what I'm pushing today is a romantic attitude
toward life. Perhaps a classical attitude toward living,
but a romantic attitude toward life. Life should be hip,
living can be square. St. Peter's is square, particularly

St. Peter's Square. I was standing at the entrance, trying to work up enthusiasm, when a small car scoots in and parks next to the fountain, from which a strong breeze is blowing water to one side. The car's windows are wound up tight, no one gets in or out, the water is splashing over it, and after a few minutes it scoots away. As it passed me I realized the driver had gotten himself a free carwash. We feel the same about St. Peter's, that driver and I. Then I walked to the Borghese Gardens and on the way I crossed the Tiber thrice. For once upon a raw and gusty day, remember, the troubled Tiber chafing at her shores, Caesar said to me, dar'st thou, Cassius, now leap in with me into this angry flood? Angry flood, I've seen more action on the Bronx River. But I like it, the earth is mastered here, nothing in extreme, but how would Shakespeare know that, no Al Italia. The little bridges were delicious, and then the Borghese Gardens, which is what I'll dream about in the better nights of my old age, unattended, patches of grass brown from the sun, which must be fierce in midsummer, serious children bouncing balls while smiling nurses watch. Children dour and adults gay, just the opposite of America. Well, I walked and walked, as I've done here every day, and at the far side of the park I came to an elaborate outdoor restaurant, deserted except for one lounging waiter. I asked him for a Coca-Cola, he had it, but it would cost me almost a buck. Why not go out of the park across the street to the stand and get a bottle of wine, he said. I did, for a quarter, took it back and lay down in the shade of a pine tree. As the sun moved I edged into the shade again, but finally I fell asleep full of vino rosso and cielo azzuro, and when I woke I was boiled, wet with sweat and contentment. My little sleep had fixed Rome in my head, developed it like an image on film, and I poured what was left of the wine into the ground and said Dei, optimi Romae dei, urbem vestram amo, revenire volo, reddite me hoc pro pietate mea, which last phrase Harvey always quotes, and may I fare better than Catullus. Then on the way back to the hotel I walked down the Spanish Steps. I didn't know they were the Spanish Steps. I mean, I didn't even know they were a thing, I just happened to walk down them, and at the bottom I turned around and they filled me with peace. I was reassured because someone had made something so nice. That's what's been so great about Rome, I've just walked around and looked, and all these triumphs of artifice have been my own discoveries. Across the street from the steps I sat down at a little white round table in the shade and began ordering cafe nero. After the third, the waiter wagged his finger at me, put his hand over his heart and flapped it like the wing of a bird. How had he known, except that Italians know everything human. I switched to Strega, which he approved of, and so I sat on and watched. Cars and motor bikes, shoppers and tourists, and every now and then I would hear the unspeakable squawk of Americans. Gawky and inept among the smooth compact wops. O they weren't the burlesque visitors of the cameras and sport shirts, but they seemed to be missing the point. They were sightseeing, they hadn't committed themselves to the spirit of the place. Probably I looked the same to them. Anyway, I was working up some anti-American mots, when a young woman—she looked like a gypsy—came begging among the tables. Her face was blasted, like faces in a nuthouse, she was great-pregnant, and she carried a baby girl in her arms. At her side was a six- or seven-year-old boy squeezing a concertina, making noise but no music. The baby girl's face was dirty and impassive, and the boy's was the face of a confused adult. Well, the three of them, and the fourth in the belly of the woman, approached a mustached Italian at another table. The beggars looked at him like people in a burning building might look at outsiders, and he smiled, was amused, and waved them on. They came toward me. I glanced up at my waiter—the guy who had warned me off the fourth cafe nero—and he too smiled and was amused. Well, I gave the woman all the change I had, which I guess was a lot, because when I buy something, instead of counting out the money, I present a big bill, and then the most terrible thing, she was so far gone in her debasement that she took the money with no sign. It's a small enough thing to say about the States, but let me say it, no American could have sat there like the Italian customer, or stood there like the Italian waiter, and smiled. In one of your own anti-American moods you said that America made nothing best. With all our wealth and activity we made nothing best. At the time I could only defend us by saying that we made drugs best. But there's something else, kid, hearts. When I got back to the hotel, the porter told me that, as usual, he had called the place in Venice and they said that Prudence had stopped over last night and gone on to a town called Bardolino on Lago di Garda. So this afternoon I'm shoving off for an Italian resort I never heard of, on an Italian lake I never heard of. Bardolino on Lago di Garda. Say it to yourself. The way the porter says it, your ass would drop off. You will like it there, he says, and nods deeply. He's a sweet guy, the one I've talked to most about how I love beautiful Rome and beautiful Italians. Every time I mention the beautiful Italians, he feels impelled to confess that he comes from Trieste, as if not to claim my admiration unjustly. O let me tell you a funny thing. He loves America because of Revelation Tobacco. It's very expensive in Italy, he explained, but he regularly puts money aside for it. What an exchange, I give him Revelation Tobacco and he gives me Rome. You will enjoy Lago di Garda, he says, and I guess I will. Not more than Rome, though. Wherever I go in my lifetime and whatever I see, this will be my first love. I'll tell you why. Having seen Rome, I know that I have someplace to go. In America I lived in my head, in my bed, in my bath, in my room. Chicago, Los Angeles, Philadelphia, Hattiesburg, never meant a thing to me. America mixed me up, put me down, spilled me out, wherever I was in it. Only the neighborhood where I was born and brought up did I like, otherwise America was cold and strange to me. And this is where I want to be, among these brown people and faded stones, under this rich sky. Yes, even if, despite my prayer, I never come here again, Rome will always be where I want to be.

✄ ✄ ✄ ✄ ✄ ✄ PRUDENCE IS GETTING married and not to me. As I checked out of Signor Martello's hotel, distributing gratuities in grand American fashion——three half-pound tins of Revelation to the porter——I received in return a fat stamp-bright envelope from the States. Enclosed was a short and enigmatic letter from Jose announcing that he and his tootsie nun were getting married. Enclosed also in the enevelope was another envelope, which quaintly had been sent to me nine days before from Venice. Inside this second envelope was a long unenigmatic letter from Prudence, which announced that she was getting married to, who else, the enterprising father of her unborn, Apparently Father had had a change of heart and full of honorable impulses flown to Italy and his love on wings of steel. I would quote this letter to you, because it was a very beautiful letter, which spoke of foregoing the private need and selfish impulse, but I tore it up and let the bits fall on Ciampino airfield. I tore and tore until the pieces were too small to hold and tear again. And I got on the plane, as planned, and flew to Milano, and I got on a bus, as planned, and rode to Bardolino, and all the while I wondered who he was, this happy fructifier. Do you know who I thought he was? Just as surely as I had leukemia two weeks ago, he was Harvey. The evidence was over-whelming. Harvey had worked at MUI before me, thus he knew Prudence before I had. And! When he learned that I was going with her he had made no comment—studiously made no comment. And! He was meeting her at Bardolino. On Lago di Garda. When I had looked up Bardolino in the Nagel guidebook, I noticed there was a town nearby named Sirmione, the modern counter-part of Sirmio, where Catullus was supposed to have kept a villa two millennia ago. It was exactly, but exactly, Harvey to choose for a rendezvous a place which held arcane meanings. Or if not the place itself, a place nearby. Then suddenly the evidence would crumble and I became sure it was Mr. Pudgybald. Neuter nonentity indeed. The smooth seducer had only pretended to pay court to Mommie in order to screw the daughter. A classic ploy. I recalled, word for word, his comments about Prudence on our trip back to the city that night along the river. He had said she was a wonderful and sensitive woman. He hadn't called her a girl, as any man his age should have. And finally, why hadn't she told me in the restaurant who the father was? Because she was ashamed of Pudgybald, ashamed of being diddled by a plump inadequacy. As I collected, sorted and refined the evidence for both cases, they replaced one another in my head with increasing speed and certainty. By the time I arrived here at Bardolino they had merged into a Har-vey Pudgybald. But who is he really? He sells Chris-Craft motorboats to rich suburbanites, but otherwise I can't tell you. I have seen him a number of times now, stared at him intently, but I cannot describe him. I do not know if he is fat or thin, tall or short, fair or dark, coarse or fine. His lips move—I have seen them from a distance—but I do not know the words they spoke. He displaces matter, I have observed him making waves in Lago di Garda. Others note him when he scratches himself—at least I believe they do—so he reflects light truly, he is no illusion. His bathing suit bulges, consequently I deduce he pees like a man. And since it is he who knocked up my friend Prudence, I judge his tool emits on occasion more than urine. In a word a whole man, a hole man. But I cannot tell you his appearance. If someone had held him down for me and someone else had forced me to remember, I could give you something, but as it is, he's a Chinese waiter, a pigeon in the park, a black cat—merely one of a species, the species of man-shaped turd, a piece of nature filling cunts and other voids, and I wish him well, a long life, a faithful companion, worldly preferment, many orgasms of exquisite strength, a deathbed repentance and eternal happiness in the afterlife. And why am I so generous? Because I am a Christian, reared to neighbor-love and cheek-turning, a gentle, genteel, Gentile chap withal. So Prudence is wedding Mr. Right, Mr. Right-in-there. She is doing the Right thing, so to speak. She mentioned the word Responsibility—not to my face but in the letter—and I must remember to suggest to her in future colloquies, if any, that she use it for the child. And perhaps when the child's confirmed she can add Accommodation. Responsibility Accommodation dear, why are you so pale, made in a hot night on the leatherette seat of a stalled auto, deserted in gestation, rejoined from guilt, born in doubt, raised in discomforture, why so pale? Stretch yourself on the couch, Responsibility Accommodation, and remember what you never knew, that Daddie meant, he really meant, to pull out, break it off, you off, ah but the warm weather, the full moon, the odds against you gathered to make his stick stick, and all those eager spermies scurried like ladies at a sale. Plunk went the winner into the soft ovum, plunk, set for life. And Mommie didn't douche you, jolt you, gouge you, shake you, did she? So don't feel bad. Daddie came to Bardolino to shower you with further icky sperm. Isn't that a sign of love? I arrived in Bardolino well after dinner and rose late the next day so that I missed them for breakfast. It wasn't until lunch that we saw one another. A picture, tanned and smiling, the four of them—Prudence, Mrs., sister Billy, friend-and-father—all seated neatly at their table under the vine-covered trellises next to the lake. As I asked the captain for my table, she saw me, half rose. But I held up my hand, turned my back. Seated I looked again, and she too was seated, staring at her plate. I found out later, when she came to my room, that at that moment she thought I had flown from the States in response to her Venice letter, and I might have. We ate, six or seven tables apart. I out-ate them, and they left, no one but Prudence knowing and she not telling, all smiling except Prudence, and then I left too. In the afternoon I went to the hotel's private dock, and they were there, Prudence bikinied in the Bardolino mode, and I watched them from the awninged bar at the foot of the dock until they left, then I swam. The water was warm and felt dirty but was as clear as a new bath. The bottom is slippery stone, little fishes nibble at the hairs on your legs. In a while she came back to the dock alone. I stayed in the water far out, looking at her. She waited, not moving, and finally dove in. I swam away, out toward the center of the lake. She didn't follow but got back on the dock and left. At four-thirty a melancholy chill sets in here, but I stayed on, floating and swimming for more than an hour, almost to abuse myself, to draw the discomfort out from the bones to the skin. And I took my time getting back and dressing so that they were gone from the dining room when I arrived. There's nothing to do in the evenings but walk or sit in the piazza, talk and drink, and I stayed in my room and waited, waited with a vengeance, and then at twelve-thirty she came. I considered letting her knock-and-whisper, but also I was eager for the scene. I opened without a word, she came in without a word. I motioned to a chair, she sat down. I wanted her to talk first, but she wouldn't, and we sat, and I watched her fine skin with the two pink spots over cheek and cheekbone. The feeling against her drained away finally because I saw I had no right to it. You won't believe this, you'll think it's sour grapes, but I didn't come to Italy to marry her necessarily, or even to confirm the engagement. I came to see, to make up my mind as my mind made up me. And there was this. If Prudence's friend had not shown, and I had decided I didn't want to marry her I would have had no feeling for her feelings. You don't think I'm that much of a prick, do you? Well, don't be fooled by me being the hero of my own letters. I am that much of a prick. Let me remind you that back at the ranch Mary thinks I'm engaged to her again. Have I wasted sympathy on Mary? Anyway, I figured all this out with Prudence on a chair, me on the bed, looking at one another between midnight and one o'clock in a hotel on Lago di Garda, and I finally gathered up the revelations and worked them into a civilized statement. I said I'm glad things are working out this way for you, Prudence. Then with a word she knocked me down. I know you are, she said. She knew I was, she really thought I was glad. I wasn't glad. I could have broken her in two just to keep her from that guy, but she thought I was glad, she was giving me credit for a generosity I'm no more capable of than I'm capable of biting off my hand. But do you see, that's why I wanted her, I wanted her because that's the way she is. But do you see also, that's why I didn't want her, why I didn't grab her back in the States, answer her letter, rush to Italy, because she thought I was something I was not. I'm Fox, Wally, Feldshuh, Austin, Foxshuh, Madam Fox, Jose, and all the rest, but this was Prudence, and if I had married her, there would have been, one dark night or one bright morning over coffee by the window, that terrible unveiling. The skin would have been pulled all the way back on prick me. Well, we talked, and she wanted me to meet this creep. It was a reasonable impulse, but I said Why, so you can include my image in his? Do you want me to approve of him or something? Well, I don't want to meet that son of a bitch, and I'm sure that son of a bitch wouldn't want to meet me. And all I did by saying this was make her sad. She excused me, said I was upset, and I was, and I tried to kiss her before she left, and she gave me her cheek instead of her mouth because she was marrying someone else and she left, and I started crying. Later I fell asleep, but I kept waking up to cry. Slob extraordinary. The next morning I watched them from my window, a boy loading luggage on the handtruck, everyone smiling, even Prudence. She didn't look up, she must have known I was there, but she didn't. She was marrying the father of her child, doing the right thing, which gives one stuff, doesn't it? I tried to see what he was like, but his face was mushed like a Francis Bacon painting. I think he had a thin mustache, but I'm not sure.

❈ ❈ ❈ ❈ ❈ ❈ ❈ ❈ ❈ I WENT TO THE post office this morning to look for mail. There was none, you bastard, and when I came out into the brilliant sunlight I felt dizzy. It was coolish, so it wasn't the weather, but I suddenly sensed that I was three thousand miles away. What I was away from I don't know, but it was three thousand miles, and I felt like a child that had been lost or abandoned by his parents. I went back into the post office, and the clerk smiled at me. Smiling wops, I thought, but for his benefit I slapped my pocket as if I had forgotten something, smiled back and left. It got worse, the world was spinning under me—spinning as it really does—but now I could feel it. I thought I might fall over, so I tried to walk, and luckily, by going slowly and keeping my legs apart I got to the church, an ancient beat-up building no bigger than a chapel. An old guy, a layman, was fussing around the altar. I asked him for the priest. Whatever priest is in Italian, I just said Priest, and he came back with a skinny dark man who looked annoyed but willing to listen. I went down on my knees right in the center aisle. Any Irish cleric would have played it like Italian opera and become a small Jesus, but this guy rubbed one hand over his forehead and with the other picked me up by the elbow and pushed me into a pew. He sat down beside me and by turning his profile adopted the manner of the confessor. The sexton came close to observe the proceedings. I didn't care, it seemed like it should be a group effort anyway. Do you speak English, Father, I said to the priest. He nodded, but obviously he didn't. Do you speak English, I said, turning to the sexton. He nodded too. OK, bless me, Father, I don't believe in what you represent, but I believe in you. Do you understand that? He nodded. I think the Church is a lot of shit, really, but it has a piece of me marked out. He nodded. I want to confess that I have been inadequate in my life, I haven't produced what the world has required of me, not what my father required, or my mother, or my employer, or my friends, or what I have required of myself, even. This is a terrible sin, do you understand? He nodded. Are you sure you don't understand English, I said to the sexton, who was surprised at being addressed again and nodded solemnly in response. Maybe most of all I didn't produce what your own organization required of me, Father. In defense of myself I can say that I tried very hard, but I think that different groups and people asked contradictory things of me. He nodded. I did satisfy my schools, though, and my new doctor thinks I'm all right and will be all right, and some of my friends do, too, I think. I say this in the spirit of evidence, not as justification, do you understand? And he nodded. I've done certain things, which have made me a certain thing. I mean that a lot of my future is already determined, so that I can't make any sweeping promises, and that's all I have to say. He turned his serious dark face to me as if to make sure that I was done, and I thought as I looked at him that this was a whore of the soul, a wonderful whore of the soul, because he was going to give me what I wanted. I want you to forgive me to the extent that you can, for all my inadequacies, and I held up my hands to indicate that that was that. He moved right into Latin, which sounded like Italian, but I heard the words Ego te absolvo, and this was a great giving, I can tell you, because the guy didn't know what I had said, I could have just come from Rome after killing the Pope, but Ego te absolvo, he said, and he looked at me again to make sure there was nothing else. Grazie, I said. He nodded a final time, got up and went whence he came. The sexton returned to his dusting or whatever, and out in the sun it was gone, I had my earth legs back. And more. The colors of the sky and the road and the faded stones and the great quiet lake, which I could see down the side streets, looked deep and rich. I felt more like a child than at any time since I was a child. Jesus, I was hungry and horny, I wanted to write books and play tennis and see movies, only all at once, so since they were serving at the hotel, I settled for lunch of soup and fish and salad and vino blanco. During previous meals I had noticed that a Hollandaise lady, of about thirty years, was also seated alone. Our eyes had met six, seven times, and after Prudence left I had secreted her image in my head like a gumdrop under the gum. Our eyes met again, but there was a big rosy famishedness about her that had and continued to put me off. Perhaps at dinner I would ask the captain to see if I could join her, but now I wanted to consolidate my new position. I would eat, go up for a siesta, swim in the afternoon, dress sweet for dinner and see. When I got to my room, however, the chambermaiden, a tiny girl and fair, was tidying. We, too, had noticed one another. As I came in she made to leave, but I smiled the smile of Italy and motioned her to go on. I flopped on the bed and watched. She seemed to be doing her work so slowly. Was I falling asleep, or was she lingering? Time almost stopped, and I felt I was in a crib, this was my nursemaid. I was three thousand miles away, wasn't the chambermaiden preparing something nice for me in consolation? A bottle? Or would she put a blanket on me? Then suddenly she seemed finished. But she had not done the nice thing. My eyes were half closed, I motioned to her with my hand. The childish part of me knew that she would come, the adult part that she wouldn't. But she did, she came to the foot of the bed. I must do something else to keep her. If I go on lying here she will leave. I had to rouse myself. Like lifting many pounds I sat up. I must do still more. I shinnied down to the foot of the bed. Still more. I slid onto my knees. My head came between her breasts, she was that tiny. So I sat back on my heels. I put my arms around her legs and pressed my face into her dress. I rubbed my nose and forehead against her and could feel the hair through her clothes. Was I frightening her? I was afraid to look up to find out. I so wanted her to stay, and by being a child, I thought, I could keep her. She wouldn't desert a child. I heard the hairs scratching against one another and against the skirt as I rubbed with my forehead. Hello, coozie, I said. The chamber-maiden said something irrelevant far above me. I'm talking to the coozie, I said, I'll talk to you later. You up there, before you fly away like a bird or pull away like a woman, I first want to say something to the coozie. I want to say that you are my one true friend, who never did me any wrong, and however your owner feels about me up there, I know you like me, don't you, crazy crack, don't you, crazy follicles? Crazy bone, I love you, I said, and put my hands and arms under the back of her skirt. She had no pants on. Her little white blouse had long sleeves and a high bodice, but she had no pants on. Her tiny ass was taut to my touch, but I loved it so much that it finally relaxed. I'm going to take a picture, I said, you won't be frightened if I take a picture, will you? And her mouth said something in Italian, so I pulled the front of her skirt over my head and closed my eyes to complete the darkness. I pressed my nose between her legs and up against the bone, her hair was in my eyes. I nuzzled her like a dog. She spread her feet slightly and in my darkness I licked her, crouching down, bending my head back. I could hear her voice, saying words or making sounds, but it was out in the light far away. I was with my friend, and whatever was going on in the owner's head didn't matter so long as she didn't take my friend away. Well, I drank my chambermaiden, I ate the rose. Her legs were shaking so, I thought she'd fall, and finally she put her hands under my arms and lifted me up. It was like growing from infancy, and she was a tiny girl again, her eyes on a level with my chest. I bent down and kissed her, and she tasted herself in my mouth. We both came together. She couldn't stay long, which struck me as ironic. Here I was, a guest, every wish realized, and my chambermaiden, whom I would so dearly have wished to keep with me, had to run off to change towels. Her name is Ermina, she lives here year around with Mommie and Daddie, two brothers and two sisters. The family has been in Bardolino for as many generations as memory serves. Daddie was a fisherman until recent years and now works for one or another of the hotels as handyman. Her two brothers are in the Italian Navy sailing on the small fleet that plies the

ports of Lago di Garda. She says they are very handsome, which I do not doubt, Italy puts the flower of its
youth into the transportation services. Her sisters are
younger than she and still go to school. Ermina works
for only five months a year, since Bardolino is a warm-
weather resort. The rest of the year she helps her mother,
at what I couldn't make out with my pocket dictionary.
I wanted to discover other things, though. Whether she
plans to stay in Bardolino, and why she went to bed with
me, but we couldn't get across to one another. She's coming back after dinner. This afternoon I'm going to the
dock for a late swim, while she helps out in the kitchen.
Jesus. She explained with the help of my watch that
she'll have to leave by nine-thirty or Daddie will be
angry. He doesn't mind her working, she said, but he
distrusts the northern Europeans who come to Bardolino
in the fall and summer—the French, Dutch, English, and
especially the Germans. No one who distrusts the Germans
can be all bad, I thought. What about the Americans, I
said. Everybody likes the Americans, she said.

✕ ✕ ✕ ✕ ✕ ✕ FOUR LETTERS, FOUR.
My mother wants to know if I'm eating my greens and
getting my sleep. Mary meaningfully inquires why, of
all countries in the world, I chose to visit Italy, the cradle

of Christianity. You I am most deeply pleased to hear from. I have charmed you back with my wit and wisdom. Jose reports that he is living in exquisite circumstances with his nun. She is afraid to be left alone, the other nuns may come and get her. She also insists that Jose not touch her until they are married. The room, he claims, is becoming too small for the three of them, his tootsie, himself and his member. The other night he put it out the window, for relief and so that tootsie could move the couch, and six pigeons immediately flew down from the roof to peck at it. Jose also said that Harvey once again is scheduled to marry Mrs. Fox. In honor of the occasion he wrote a Very Tale. It seems that once upon a time there was a thirteen-year-old prodigy named Sonny, who had not only mastered the disciplines of chemistry, biology, astronomy, physics, mathematics and psychology, but had made substantial contributions to the fields as well. The most remarkable of these was his cure for the Oedipus complex. It seems that in a lot near his house the youthful genius built a space capsule capable of carrying a man ten light years from earth and back again—at the speed of light. Naturally scientists all over the world were eager to know the details of the machine, but Sonny took into his confidence only his beloved mother. Finally when the day of the machine's first test arrived, instead of the festive air usually attending such events, the boy stipulated that only his mother be present. The announced plan was for him to go off into space by himself, but under the guise of showing his mother the interior of the craft, he locked her inside and pressed the launching button. His father was furious, the public was stunned, and if it had not been that Sonny was under age the government would have taken legal action against him. As it was, the world could only sit back and wait for the periodic reports Sonny issued from the blockhouse about the capsule's progress. Everything was going on schedule, according to Sonny, and since no one had any way to check, they had to take his word for it. Well, time passed, and Sonny became a man. He was now twenty-three. The capsule had been out in space ten years, and sure enough, Sonny issued a report that at last the craft had reached the height of its arc and was beginning its return to earth. All this time, of course, Sonny was making important discoveries in the other sciences. From ages sixteen to twenty-three he had received eight consecutive Nobel Prizes. Well, more time passed, and twenty years to the day after the original launching the capsule landed safe and sound in a small lake a mile from Sonny's house. Out stepped his mother, refreshed and rested, and wondrous to behold she looked no older than the day she had left. Sonny himself was now thirty-three. Time had elapsed normally for him but had stood still for the mother because she was traveling at the speed of light. The entire world was thrilled at this dramatic confirmation of the theory of relativity. Sonny, however, was disappointed. He had never doubted the theory of relativity, he had set about to seek a cure for the Oedipus complex. And now when he looked at his mother's slim figure and youthful face he realized to his dismay that his Oedipal yearnings demanded not a contemporary but a woman twenty years older than himself. For weeks he was despondent and inactive. Men acclaimed him the greatest genius history had ever known, but it meant nothing to him. Then one day he realized that all was not lost. Swiftly he fashioned another capsule like the first and launched himself into space. Twenty years to the day after leaving he landed in the self-same lake near his home. On emerging from the craft he appeared to be thirty-three, since time for twenty years had stood still for him. Now his mother was fifty-three, however, and his heart went out to her, just as it had all through his adolescence. And since his father had died twelve years before, an old and embittered man, there was nothing and no one to stand in his way. With a fury of application he fashioned still another capsule, this one built to accommodate two people, and one warm summer night he launched his mother and himself into space at the speed of light. Apparently the machine was constructed not to return to earth because it was never heard from again, and it is assumed that Sonny and his mother lived happily ever after. Jose added that I have written so appreciatively of Europe that he fully forgives me everything. He explained that he was nice to me only because I had been sick, but he harbored resentments. Now he even apologizes for suspecting I was a Jew. No Jew could love Europe as I do, he said, no Jew can love anything. When I get back I'll tell him about Jesus, but do I love Europe so much? I wonder. I told you how, before I got here, I thought Europe would be a bust. In what way, I didn't know, maybe just dirty and corrupt. My mother thinks Europe is dirty and corrupt, my father thought so too. A thousand times I heard them talking with outrage about World War II, nice American boys dying in and for cynical Europe. My parents were deepdown isolationists. It was OK to feed Europe—obviously Europeans couldn't take care of themselves—but like George Washington said, we ought to stay clear of foreign entanglements. And this made sense to me, makes sense to me now, but I drew a mean picture from these and other domestic sentiments. Even the Europeans my parents met among their neighbors rubbed them wrong. Ungracious guests, full of airs and condescensions. Now that I've seen a little of Europe I understand the condescension. More important, though, I understand, I think, America's distrust of Europe. It starts in grammar school with the Pilgrim bit, the fled idealists, and it follows with the heroes, adventurers, downtrodden but enterprising stock that had the guts, sense and strength to cross an ocean, learn a language, clear a field, kill an Indian. Take you, don't you nourish an inmost prejudice that everyone who came to America did right, especially Columbus? Nothing else was ever suggested, the contrary never considered. High-domed or beetle-browed, out of England on the Mayflower or out of Russia on a cattleboat, those emigrants were pluckie, lucky worthies. And maybe they were. My father's father's father shipped from Liverpool in 1862 at sixteen and joined the Union Army in New York for a two-hundred-buck consideration, which was to be his stake. I have one of his medals in my bag. His older brother, nineteen, came with him, got off the boat before the others to take the lay of the land, met rooming-house agents passing out handbills on the dock. He gathered them up, went back on board and sold them to his fellow immigrants as room reservations for a buck apiece. That story was told to me in sly pride, as, in a sense, I tell it to you now. It represents American enterprise, and I bought it as such. But my point is this: if the free, brave and enterprising came to America, who stayed in Europe? Why, the bondaged, indolent and cowardly—excepting, of course, those few smarties who exploited all the others. You know, the smarties who start wars and all that. Wait, I'm not done. Consider our immigration laws. From what both the proponents and the adversaries of these laws say, you gather that all the world wants to crawl into our nest. Is this so, would the average Roman forsake his evening stroll along the Via Veneto for the Fifth Avenue Easter Parade? A month ago I'd have said Of course. And I myself don't even like Fifth Avenue, that's the wildest part of this American illusion. Well, I will say in my own defense that it took me only five minutes on Rome streets to discover Europe, although it took me till today to discover America. I got my hair cut. The barber was a young, younger than I, good-looking, fair wop. He spoke English, also French and German—the tourist languages of Bardolino. Well, I was full of Italy, I'd just come from breakfast and a swim, not at the dock, but from the garden under one of my windows. I'm not in the hotel proper, you know, I'm in an annex across an alleyway from the main building.

The annex is a converted ten-room nineteenth-century summer home. Mornings, instead of weeing and washing and brushing my teeth, I put on a bathing suit and go barefoot down the marble stairs, over the pebble-covered path through the garden to the six stone steps which descend into Lago di Garda. I float around, no one in sight, until I've washed off the night, then wander to one of the tiny white round tables outside the hotel proper for panini, shell-shaped butter, marmalade and cafe nero. Each morning a different waiter pulls this duty, always in a bad mood, not surly but frowning. The poor buggers work right through supper, which ends at nine, get one day off a week, when they try to make out with the unattached lady guests. Well, I was full of Italy, full of the early sun and quiet hustle of the help, and when this barber spoke to me in English I tried to tell him how very bella his Italia was. I laid it on, and I got nothing for it. I watched him in the mirror, nothing. Was Italy so precious that praise from an outsider was a profanation? No, man. The poor slob wanted to go to America. It was O. Henry. I suspected at first that he was discontent because he didn't like barbering, but, no, barbering was a good job, he intended to barber in San Francisco. Why San Francisco? Then it came out. The guy wanted a car, and if he stayed in Italy he wouldn't have a car for many years. His uncle, who was a builder in San Francisco, not only had his own car, but was buying his daughter one for her next birthday. What could I say? Here was this multilingual, attractive young man living in a North Italian resort town that looked to me like paradise, and he was talking like an African primitive. I asked him again about the barbering. No, not only was barbering a good job, barbering in Bardolino was a prize, he had the job only because of his languages. Why a prize? The question was indiscreet, but he answered: because of the tips. After the haircut I asked him to have a coffee with me next door, and he in turn asked the boss, a black dago, who agreed only because I was a customer. Over coffee he explained more. Italy is very beautiful, that's why all Europe comes here in the summer, but it is more beautiful to a rich man like myself than to a poor man like him. He opened the shop at eight in the morning and closed it at seven-thirty in the evening, he worked six days a week, and on Sunday helped his father in the lemon grove. I asked him if he ever considered going to a university, and he told me that his grades had not been good enough. But you know four languages, I said, and he shrugged as a child might if you remarked that he knew how to jump rope. Everyone in the shops here, he explained, knows languages. Well, we didn't get through to one another. I looked like a rich man to him—although he wouldn't take a tip from me because I had treated him to a cafe nero—and he looked like a sick man to me, suffering from materiosis. Yet he wanted a car, it was Gogol's overcoat, who can say it nay? If I had my Austin-Healey with me, I'd give it to him, so he could have his Italy too. And I thought to myself, what would my father have been here? A successful salesman who could send his son to a good school? Not likely. More probably a mail clerk, a barber, the owner of a barbershop maybe, or maybe like my chambermaiden's father a handyman and ex-fisherman. And what about me? I'd have been what he was. There is no mark on me that would have obtained me preferment. I'm no brighter than the barber with his four languages, no more personable. Ah, you say, is what I have so much better? Yes, I think it is. I'm not fixed. Because I swim off a private dock, eat lunch under vine leaves, treat him to cafe nero, the barber thinks I'm a rich man. It all costs fifteen bucks a day, but for the extent of my stay here I'm a rich man. When I get back to the States? At worst I'll get a job in what my old lady calls a large organization. At best I'll be a Writer, wordwinder, one of the elite of my time. These are the limits of my possibilities, and anything within them is better than cutting hair in Bardolino, or San Francisco. That's my discovery of America, my personal economic discovery of America. I don't like the weather there or the architecture or the faces, but it has gifted me with this, and I am grateful. In exchange I'll rise to the Star-Spangled Banner, vote, bear arms, and attend America's destiny. Big deal, you say. Yes, it is. I was brought up a Catholic, not an American. I was taught to be a creature of God, not the citizen of a country, and for me this is a big deal, a pact of import. But enough patriotism.

❧ ❧ ❧ ❧ ❧ ❧ ❧ ❧ ❧ I JUST SNUCK away from Jose's room. He's giving a sort of coming-out party for Rita-Barbara, nun-tootsie, which I've decided to contract to nutsie. The place is loaded, it's like a submarine running out of oxygen. I never suspected Jose had so many friends, all sorts, smoothies, strays, unescorted wildly handsome chicks, Harvey stoned—most of them, as far as I can gather, with literary connections. But the hit is the nutsie, everyone is attracted to her nun-tootsiness. She reminds me of a layer of white paint on black. From an angle the surface looks white. Straight on, you can see black underneath. She's a miracle of happy happenstance, nun's short hair becomes a chic bob, her lack of makeup is voguish, simplicity of dress high style, shyness and silence wise amusement. I saw more than one big-city boyo, drink and cigarette in hand, sizing her up from the corner, thinking his answer might lie on the thigh of this mysterious little pussycat. And it might too. She must have a perfect body, there is a fineness about the tendons of her ankles and a subtle firm swell in the little forearms that speaks an exquisite combination of soft and hard. A fag in there told me that he'd like to hollow her out to make a candybox. Her head no one seems to know for sure, not even Jose, who is smit but mystified. He says that she is willing to marry him, but must first get a release from her vows, which I gather is possible since they weren't final. Anyway, that's not what I came away to say. I met a tall classy jane in there named Peggy, who said that Jose had told her I was a writer. She's an editor, and what kind of writer am I? A novelist, I said boldly. Well, one thing led to another, and I have promised to deliver the manuscript of my first book to her in two weeks. My idea at the moment was to sit down once again and push Austin to his final reward. But I can't do that. I've had Austin, Austin me. So here's my idea. If you've kept my letters, send them back, I'll retype them and claim they make an epistolary novel. Sounds great, doesn't it, epistolary novel. And why not? Even if it's dull, no one will be able to deny it's a characterization of a guy writing letters. Hey, I've got another idea. Suppose I leave everyone's name in. The publisher will be smothered with lawsuits. I'm judgment proof, being nearly broke, but the publisher is probably loaded. Everybody can sue. Fox, Mrs. Fox, Rita maybe, Jose. I'll have stolen his Very Tales. He can sue like crazy. Harvey, Feldshuh. Prudence could sue. If I put the chambermaiden's last name in, she can sue. That would be great. It's Ermina Flagello, resident of Bardolino. Who else? Dr. Curtin. You could sue, I guess. I tell you what, if you want to sue, leave in all the stuff about yourself. If not, cross it out. Wally can sue. Christ, here's another idea. After everybody collects from the publisher, we take the money—I expect you all to support me as the source of these goodies—and we form an ideal community at Montauk Point or New Hope or Bardolino or somewhere. I think I'll change Mrs. Frank's name. I couldn't stand her kid. No, I'll leave it in, it's only fair, but we won't invite her. Hey, I think I'll include this letter, send this letter back with the others, it will put the publisher off his guard. What do you think, do you think I can get away with it? I don't mean the lawsuits, I mean passing the letters off as a novel. I can see the reviews. If it bores my readers to hear me inveigh at least once a fortnight against the tawdry, the inept and the sensational in current fiction, I must explain that it bores me no less. It bores, bores, bores me. Someone, however, must speak the truth about the trash that is foisted on the public today in the name of literature. This is a small volume, described by its publishers as a novel. I have always understood a novel to be a narrative fiction of a certain length with beginning, middle and end. This book, however, has neither beginning, middle nor end, except in terms of pages that precede or follow other pages. Purporting to be a series of letters from one young man to another during the summer and early fall following their graduation from college, it is no more than hastily written and often foul anecdotes intermixed with vague and pretentious observations about life. I gather the author intended these letters to recount the passage of his hero from adolescence to a manhood of sorts. If they had been meant to convey a picture of a mixed-up American youngster, I would say they had some merit, but nowhere is there the slightest indication that the narrator's attitudes differ from the author's. In fact, I suspect that this is largely an autobiographical book, thrown together from real letters the author wrote to a real friend. How else explain the book's inordinately abrupt and unpleasant jerkiness, or its accordion quality, which would seem to allow it to be half as long as it is as well as twice as long? Nonetheless, the book interests me, not as a created thing, but as a phenomenon, as a piece of evidence which shows what the lack of spiritual values and aesthetic tradition can and is doing to many young Americans. If the hero or author of this book were my son I would take him aside and explain to him that if he wants to interpret the contemporary American experience to his fellow man—as I rather believe this hero and author both want to do—he must first form a useful and consistent attitude toward life and second develop a means of communicating it. I would suggest that he find out who he is and what he wants, that he work out a sense of personal values, and then that he read or reread the great contemporary masters of the novelistic statement, Marquand, Cozzens, Snow. Only in this way will he deserve our attention, and only in this way will he get it. Instead he has gathered together an assemblage of tasteless and exhibitionistic oddments, some of which seem intended to titillate and others to shock. The excesses of the sexual descriptions and the gratuitous use of four-letter words, peculiarly enough, are not the most offensive ingredients of this generally offensive book. Most offensive are the frequent and irrelevant slurs on religious and national groups. Prot-

220   *charles simmons*

estants, Jews, and especially Catholics are frequently insulted, as are Italians, Negroes, Irish, Germans and Americans. There is even, in the last section of the book, a harsh mock review of the book itself, intended, I imagine, to disarm criticism. Well, it fails entirely. Many is the book reviewer, I suspect, who, like myself, will see in it his own distaste articulated. In fact, I am now quoting, word for word, from the same mock review. You know, one thing is worrying me—me me, that is— I really ought to tie up all the loose ends. Take Austin. Suppose I send him one night walking along the shore near his parents' bungalow. He's become a wild animal almost, and suppose he sees a beach party in progress, people his own age having a good time. He's been considering swimming out into the ocean to drown himself, but the sight of all this youth and gaiety attracts him. The youngsters are playing a game, they have blankets over their heads and are stumbling around trying to catch and identify one another. Austin puts himself in the way of a girl who has wandered from the group. She takes hold of him through the blanket but can't guess who he is, even though they talk. Austin feels this is the first human contact he has made in his whole life. Finally the girl throws the blanket off and, of course, sees nothing. She thinks he has run into the night. Actually he is standing beside her, watching her beautiful face just barely lit by the distant fire. He leaves her, however, walks along the beach, and hours later, as dawn comes up, finds his floggis washed in with the sea shells, eats it and becomes opaque again. In his nakedness he runs back to his house and now is determined to seek out the girl from the beach party. I thought up this ending some time ago and tried it out on Jose. He said it was fine. If a writer wants to end a novel happily, he said, he shouldn't solve the hero's problems—that would be unrealistic—he should merely indicate hope. OK, that's done. Now how about me? Well, let's see, if you've kept the letters and if the publisher buys them, I'll marry Mary. For me she's better than Prudence. She knows I'm faulted. Not as an individual, but out of principle. She understands that I'm a victim, like herself, of original sin. There won't be any disillusionment over coffee one morning. And if we have trouble, I can always write those nasty little marital stories you see around. Jose? Jose will marry his nun in a civil ceremony, but years and years pass before she can obtain release from her vows, during which time they live together-apart. Material for his greatest Very Tale. Harvey? Harvey I don't know. O let's say he does marry Mrs. Fox and they make it. Things have to work out for somebody.

For a complete list of books available from Penguin in the United States, write to Dept. DG, Penguin Books, 299 Murray Hill Parkway, East Rutherford, New Jersey 07073.

For a complete list of books available from Penguin in Canada, write to Penguin Books Canada Limited, 2801 John Street, Markham, Ontario L3R 1B4.